FREAKING OUT

the Novel

by
helmut schonwalder

FREAKING OUT
the Novel

With & About Roxi The Waitress...
...and her bouts with...
...HI, so-called human intelligence
&
AI, aka artificial intelligence!

My **Roxi books** are works of fiction.

The names, characters, businesses, places, events, and incidents are either the product of the author's imagination or used in a fictitious manner.
Any resemblance to real living or dead persons is purely coincidental.

I used real places and local Central Coast landmarks in my descriptions, to create appropriate settings and surroundings for this Roxi book.

The character Roxi in the Roxi books is also entirely fictional.

My imagined Roxi does, however, abide by known facts in the author's life about his travels and a life lived in hotels and restaurants.

helmut s.

Index

Chapter 1
60 DAY NOTICE TO VACATE

Roxi parked her car, an older blue and white Volkswagen Bus, she had lovingly named Mathilda, on the street. She planned to be ready to pick up another fare as soon as her iPhone rang. For all her calls as a driver for PickMeUp, a rideshare company, she had it set for a distinct ring, the noise of a race-car revving up its engine.

Walking through the parking lot towards her apartment above the carports, she asked herself, "Should I have accepted that $500 from the fat-rich guy, and visited with him at his suite at the Luxury Beach Lodge?"

Outward shaking her head, inward smiling, Roxi was proud of her good figure at her age, still looking 40ish, and her racy, hot looks. After all, that's what the foreigner, the one she had chauffeured earlier from the airport to the Luxury Beach Lodge, had called her "A very pretty, foxy, hot and racy lady!" Yes, Roxi took what he had said as a compliment at her age, nearing 65. She also needed money, but no, not him, not this way, not today. Roxi looked up and wondered what her grandma Lily, now presiding in the afterlife, would have done with and for that rich fellow.

Happy about having made her choice, feeling at peace within herself and with the world around her, all smiles, feeling young and full of energy, she darted up the stairs taking two steps at a time. Coming to a sudden stop, she stared at the piece of paper stuck with blue tape to her apartment door. She hurried, running up the remaining steps and as she got closer, breathing heavy, hearing her heart beating in her ears, she read the "60 DAY NOTICE TO VACATE" in large letters. She grabbed the paper. The painters-tape, holding the document in place, let go of the door. Entering her apartment, non-stop, she kept on reading the one single page over and over. Unable to think straight, and very angry, she slammed the door shut behind herself.

Experiencing fear of the unknown, the being abandoned, having no place to go, no relatives to stay with, she went into her bedroom and sat down on her bed. She read the 60-day notice, one more time. Roxi knew this was not possible. It couldn't be true. Telling herself, "It's a mistake." She came to a conclusion "The MacMontry family would never do this to me." She knew the landlord's family forever since childhood. Roxi grew up with their kids. She went to school with Frank, the landlord's son.

Her smartphone interrupted all thoughts with the sound of revving race car engines. She let it go to voicemail. Someone needed a ride. It was followed up by the typewriter noise, associated with messages arriving on her iPhone. The same people, who had called earlier. Foreigners, by the sound as she listened to the voice message. This could have been a good fare, driving two people up to the city.

She was uninterested because her one-track mind was still occupied with the 60-day notice. She couldn't believe what she had read, over and over. Her brain urged her, "I must solve the mystery behind that 60-day notice to vacate now." Her hand shook as she spoke to her phone: "Siri! Call the landlord!" It rang. No answer at the landlords' residence, not even the answering machine was kicking in. Then she recalled that someone had mentioned a month ago, about the MacMontrys' plans to leave town, and because of the lower taxes, moving their residence up north to Oregon. Roxi tried once more. This time Frank MacMontry's home. No luck.

Reviewing in detail the 60-day notice, Roxi realized it was not signed by but for the landlords by a Steve G.D. Zilla. Having Siri looking up his office address, she realized that yes, a Steve Zilla office was uptown, on the corner below the Automobile Association's office. While Siri was giving Roxi driving directions, shifting gears like a racecar driver, she got there in half the time as it normally would take. She may have run a red light,

overlooked a stop sign,
speed limit; nothing mat...
get her hands on this Steve
straightened out. Roxi knew ...
Siri announced: "We have
destination," she saw the sign:
Property Management. The bu...
looking like much on the outside, ...
double-doors, on the inside, Stev...
management company was rather
barely noticed the all dark wood pane...
the high ceilings, and two fans with ...
wooden blades slowly rotating, in-b...
them the large Venetian glass chandelier,
enormous size very hard to overlook.
counted three tables with Windsor style chair...
the now empty waiting area. In front of her,
bar-like raised counter and a young woman on a...
tall wooden chair, in style matching the Windsor
pattern. Behind Steve's secretary, two large
hand-carved doors, with no names or signs,
leading somewhere beyond into the company's
private hidden spaces and offices. Roxi
presented the 60-day notice, holding it up in
front of the woman's eyes, who was ignoring the
obviously upset Roxi. The young woman was
busy with an important sweetheart

conv...
at le...

an...
h...

ersation. After all, she did say "I love you!"
ast a dozen times into the phone.

Finally hanging up with a smile on her face,
d sparkling eyes, she asked Roxi, "How may I
lp you?"

Roxi's "What's this about?" lead to the
oung woman taking the paper from Roxi's hand
and reading it to her, "60-day notice..., ...that
says that you need to vacate the premises where
you live within 60 days."

She added, "When you are ready, please
give us a call so we can do the pre-moving-out
inspection, and such is a free service we offer."
With a stern face, she handed the 60-day notice
back to Roxi, who stunned, was shaking her
head. And before she could say anything else,
the receptionist in a semi-friendly inquiring tone
asked the clarifying question, "Can't you read?"

Roxi with teary eyes mumbled, "I have been
living in my apartment for over 25 years now.
Have never been late with the rent, you sure this
is no mistake?"

That's when one of those large carved
doors was pushed open from the inside. Some
lady with long red hair, wearing a partly closed
white blouse, red mini skirt, and red high heels,
appeared. And she didn't look the happy go

lucky way, more like being totally embarrassed, ashamed and flustered, as she stormed out of the office. Roxi barely noticed her, she was focusing beyond her, on the man, sitting behind a large carved desk. This was no other than the Steve she knew as Godzilla Steve. He was still smiling and waving goodbye to the long-legged, short-skirted woman. Roxi didn't hear Steve's "Bye Cindy honey, I stop by tomorrow, we'll work on it some more, you are good!" as she stormed through the open door, the 60-day notice in hand, to face the monster who had dared to interrupt her near-perfect life. Her "You signed this? What's the story behind it? Why? What did I do wrong?" was answered with laughter and a: "Good day, my friend. Roxi, dear, I was expecting to see you!" Yes, Roxi knew the guy, this Steve guy. When she saw the name on the 60 days to vacate notice, she thought it was a different Steve, a Steve G.D. Zilla. Somewhat surprised she realized, yes this was the same she knew as the fellow from the bar. She had always been under the impression that Godzilla Steve was a banker. In all his talks at the bar his topics were money, loans and interest rates, unless he talked about women.

At one of Roxi's three jobs, not counting the driving for the PickMeUp rideshare company, she worked at the Sassy Station & Bar, serving drinks and food. This week she was only scheduled for one shift at Sassy's because business was slow. During the busy months, she had done three, sometimes four shifts a week. Roxi was paying $1450 a month for her 2 bedroom apartment these days, having raised her own rent twice in the past 5 years, first from $1200 to 1300, and last year another $150. She wanted her landlord to be happy. She knew that she paid about half what others were paying for the same size of apartment lately due to an acute housing shortage, caused by severe constraints on construction of new homes, mostly because of a ridiculous complicated permit process, and the high demands for housing on the peninsula. Roxi knew she couldn't afford to pay more, not in the offseason, not at the time. The three jobs being minimum wage and tips, and the fourth job driving for the PickMeUp Company wasn't much either. It all barely added up to a $2900 income a month on average.

And there she stood. Frozen in place, listening to Steve telling her all about the MacMontry family, about their financial problems. He explained details about bankruptcy they went through, about judgments against Roxi's now former landlords. And finally that in order to square up with one of the local lenders, the MacMontry family members had signed a quitclaim deed. They had deeded the apartments over to a lender. "This lender happens to be Mr.Ventura." Was there something wrong with her hearing? Did Steve say? "My uncle needs the apartment, better get moving, the sooner and the better."

Roxi asked: "So, Mr.Ventura, your uncle is throwing me out on the street, no warning, nothing? And the MacMontry clan is gone." As she looked at him, he stared back at her, but not her face, but all over checking her out and she could feel his eyes traveling from legs up to her breast and back. No, Roxi didn't understand half of it. She knew Mr.Ventura, a VIP and close friend of the Sassy Station & Bar owner's family. Coming to think of the bar owners, she hadn't seen either one of the couple, Tony and Teddy lately. Then again, they lived in Hillsborough and having Dan in charge; their business was in good hands. Yes, Roxi had been waiting on Steve as her customer at the Sassy Station & Bar several times. She also knew Mr.Ventura, known to be a rich and ruthless investor. She clearly recalled his preferred table. He loved to sit in the retro furnished booth, the one at the very end of the bar-room, the semi-private-one, with the large comfortable bench like u-shaped couch. The one with the two small cocktail tables, and it was always reserved for him, at least for the past 10 to 12 months. Here she had witnessed his lewd behaviors. The bar manager had named it the "Ventura-Play" style. In one hand holding his smartphone, unless he was sipping on his drink, the other was under the skirt, or in the blouse, of whatever female company he had brought along that night. Roxi admitted, she was somewhat impressed by the number and variety of truly most slutty women the old geezer, and his wealth, attracted. At the one or the other occasion, Roxi had noticed Mr.Ventura and his for this night lady friend returning from the genderless bathroom together, from the "powder room." She recalled his grinning victorious smile upon entering the bar, his now-look-at-me pose, while some white dusting above her upper lips be could possibly be read as a sign of her licking or snorting some powder.

Roxi's take on it was, "At least they didn't snort cocaine in front of everyone like some guests did at the bar during the late hours." Steve's uncle seldom finished his one drink. However he made sure his female companion got as many drinks as possible. He enjoyed naughty jokes, and salacious conversations, and loved the engrossment, being fascinated by the behavior of those silly, drunk females as his company.

Steve called those, his uncle's women "cunts" and "bitches" while sitting by himself, in their company. He, just like his uncle, acted like he was busy reading messages or emails on his Samsung smartphone. Roxi had noticed Steve's watching and videotaping his uncle's indecent grab and play, in the booth right next to him. Roxi was quite sure that it was his uncle's behavior, which was rubbing off on Steve. On at least half a dozen occasions, Steve had been petting her butt too, as she leaned forward while serving drinks. And a couple of times he had told her what he would like to do and which parts of her body he likes the most. He never got what he had asked for.

Yes, she could have slapped him or poured drinks on his pants, knowing that hot coffee works best, followed with a glass of iced water. However, as a professional waitress and in need to keep her job, so she could pay rent, she had put up with Steve, and others, over the years, while working in more or less fine places. The Sassy Station & Bar used to be mainly business men, then it became a gay and lesbian bar, and during the past year it had become a hangout for drug dealers, money launderers, big and small crooks, and some street girls, there to pick up a date. Thinking about it, in the past year, neither Steve nor Mr.Ventura ever paid their bill. The manager added it to an open bar-account. At the end of her shift, when she cashed out, Dan gave her a 10% tip amount, in cash, on the total of the night's Steve and Mr.Ventura tab.

The more time Roxi spent taking this Steve guy's inventory, the less she liked him. She didn't like the Ventura guy in the first place either. She suddenly knew why people called him Steve the Monster, Godzilla Steve, and it made sense. And yes whatever he was saying went in one ear and out the other, Roxi saw his mouth moving but didn't hear much what he said, including that he plans to stop by the apartment to have a more intimate talk with her. Steve must have noticed Roxi peering at some spot on his left side next to the beautiful old carved desk. She thought it was a rag, but the more she gawked she realized that it was a small, red woman's slip. "Is that yours?" She asked pointed at the underwear. Steve picked it up and in an attempt to hand it to her said "Let's see if it fits you. Honey left me a souvenir." As she didn't answer or seem to think it was funny, Steve put the pure silk G-string on his desk. Having seen and heard enough without listening. She finally turned around and walked out of Steve's office, out of the building.

Once sitting in her Volkswagen Bus, she felt somewhat better…, …still her head was spinning. After being lectured and insulted by this Steve Godzilla, Roxi arrived home all exhausted, beat, but deep down pissed off at what this man had done to her.

*****

Steve got up, and from the front room, watched Roxi getting in her blue and white van. Turning around facing Janet, his secretary, the same was doing her best to be rather discrete by letting him know "Mr. Zilla that is a colorful pair of underwear you are wearing today."

He looked and hastily closed the buttons on his pants fly, still open since Cindy honey's visit earlier. Janet his secretary didn't know this, as she was thinking that Roxi was the lucky one. Staring at the wet spot on her bosses pants, in the same area where his underwear sported a dollar size damp area, Janet wondered what she would have to do to get a raise, because that's what she had been waiting for, it had been a long time now. Janet wasn't sure, if sitting on it or just sucking it would provide better results. She knew her boyfriend would never find out, and if her paycheck would get a lift, it surely was worth doing. But how?

Steve, unaware of Janet's plans, was looking out the windows, Roxi was gone. Yes, he had plans for her, and he was sure that it all shall work out, in time, and in his favor, after all he was a betting man, and considered himself to be a born winner. As he returned to his office, the door still open Janet followed, seeing the G-string, she commented "…nice material," and picking it up, close to her nose commenting "…that smells of some expensive French perfume…" watching his face inquiring "…don't you think so?" as she held it up close to his face. Steve's "Janet forgive me, but I feel so horny right now, does such ever happen to you?" got her "Yes me too." It was about twenty minutes later that Mr.Ventura stopped by. He didn't see Janet, ready to open his nephew's office door, he stopped, hearing the "Yeah! Yeah! Yeah! Oh Yeah, Yes!" his face was all smiles. With a big grin he sat down on Janet's seat, and it didn't take too long that she came out. Guilty was written over her face, as she said something about "...was busy taking his dictation for some legal papers." After his "The door was open so I came in. Janet you look better than ever, so hot and pretty today..." he walked into Steve's office. The same was somewhat surprised but then laughed as Mr.Ventura asked "Can I have Janet next month when my secretary takes vacation, for a week? She has such a sexy look, and nice ass. You know, her screams could be heard right out the door." Steve's "Yes that's what hump-day is all about." Got his uncle's words of approval, "You are a lucky guy."

Chapter 2
Conference Center

Roxi needed to be busy and in the company of others, being alone this evening was a recipe of feeling sorry for herself, a time of self-pity, to be absolutely miserable, a true nightmare in the making. She looked for her smartphone, then remembered she had left it in the car. Roxi went to get it.

The iPhone was in her car, somehow had landed up under the front passenger seat. Wondering whom she could call, because she needed to talk to someone, sharing her pain, the money-money song played, distinctly announcing a call from one of her job places. She answered it before being able to complete her extended trip into resentment-land or getting on and off the pity-pot. It was the banquet manager at the Triples Hotel. They needed her. They were short-handed for a large VIP dinner. His "Sorry to bother you, on so very short notice. Can you, willste please help me out? Roxi we do really need you tonight!" Roxi answered with a "Yes, dear, sure, I shall be there within the hour."

She took a shower, refreshed, put makeup on. All dressed up in black pants, white blouse, black vest and black bowtie she looked forward to working the party at the Triples Hotel & Restaurant. As Triples was just four blocks downhill from Roxi's apartment, she decided to walk. And the smartphone stayed at home, next to her Android tablet, atop the Windows laptop. It wasn't 6 o'clock yet. The city below and the blue waters of the Pacific all bathed in the early evening, late afternoon sun. Earlier in the day, she recalled seeing fog above the bay, the usual. "Where did the time go?" Roxi wondered as she walked by those older Italian dwellings on the path downtown. She wasn't Sicilian herself but had learned to love living on Spaghetti Hill.

As she got closer to the bay, closer to Triples, looking back up the hill, she heard herself saying: "I may need to let go of you, my love!"

At the hotel, she found Hans, the Banquet Manager in deep conversation with Emille the Chef de Cuisine. It was Emille whose: "Oh, Roxi mademoiselle, today you are monsieur Hans's savior." put a big smile on her face. The "...tonight's event, if we screw up, some of us shall have to look for a new job," she took as whatever it was worth, Emille and Hans were perfectionists, Roxi highly respected their abilities to adhere to the utmost highest standards in guest service.

"Ja, Roxi, danke, to come tonight. It's all set. The chef is ready, everything is ready to go, I have two bars set up, I have food runners, a break-down and clean-up-crew, and I have ten servers, five short, the party has grown from 100 to 150 people, 15 ten-tops. All I had scheduled were ten servers, well no eleven because you are here." Roxi nodded her head, trying to make him feel better said, "I take two tables, what banquet room?"

"Oh no! Mon Dieu..." Emille added, "...no, it's across the street, at the Conference Center."

Finding out that she still had over an hour to kill before the guests' arrival, Roxi walked across the street to the Conference Center. Familiar with working there conventions and meetings, she had no problem to get situated. First she checked on the setup. Fifteen tables of ten were set for a six-course dinner with all the accompanying wine glasses. All looked okay to her. Still here and there a wineglass needed polishing, silverware straightened out, salt & pepper sets waited to be refilled. Roxi was getting deeply involved in the planning, and outcome of this party, especially her two tables, it let her forget all that she had been through a few hours earlier. After hearing Hans talking about some people may lose their jobs, if this banquet was less than perfect catered, she knew it had to be a big deal, a special event. Hans was always very positive, and upbeat. She was not going to let him down. All Roxi was concentrating on was to pull off a successful dinner party, nothing less than first-class, living up to her own expectations, being willing, able and ready to do her job, as expected, like clockwork and setting a good example for all co-workers. Roxi completed the individual work-station setup, all the little stuff guests don't see but need. She went and got ice from the ice makers in the back area. Then upped the number of white wine and champagne bottles to be chilled. "Nothing worse than warm champagne!" Roxi said to herself. Next, she opened bottles of red wine, to let the wine breathe. Coffee had to be made too, extra plates, saucers, and cups needed to be stocked, sugar bowls and creamers be ready.

Lucky enough, Bernd a Swiss-trained waiter was there too. Having worked banquets for the past 30 years, he knew what was needed. Roxi was happy to see Bernd as one of the banquet servers. Bernd gladly took two tables. Obviously, he hadn't expected anything less. As the other five waitresses and four waiters arrived, they divided the remaining tables between each other and worked together to finish the station set up.

Roxi listened as one of the banquet chefs explained to the wait-staff and the food-runners, a team of 6 young waiters, what and when to pick up in the kitchen. He also made sure everyone knew what's on the menu, most important for all, was to know, "... it's simple, straightforward plate service tonight, we plate it, and you serve it!"

Hans arrived '15 minutes to show-time.' He was delighted to know all was under control.

Then he stepped outside the room and talked with the two bartenders, who had set up their bars on opposite sides of the gathering, greeting and meeting area out front the banquet room. Worried about not being able to take care of 150 people from two bars, Hans looked for Bernd and Roxi, and yes they offered to assist the bartenders and help to serve pre-dinner-drinks as needed.

Soon after, a few couples arrived, and within 15 minutes the space in front of the banquet room was filled with people from many countries. French, Spanish, Portuguese, Italian, German, Japanese, Korean and Chinese was spoken aside from the more common English, and those with South African, Australian and British accents. A melting pot of cultures. Where chit-chatting was not possible, a smile, a friendly gesture was all that was needed to communicate, as they sipped on their pre-dinner-drinks. Forty-five minutes after the first guests arrived, Hans acting as a ceremonial master opened the large doors to the dining area. By this time most people knew what table and seat were theirs, and if not, they were able to read the large lettered place-card with their names or find their table and place on one of several large seating charts on display easels. Roxi had counted seven in the reception area, and two more in the banquet room. It took the better part of 15 minutes until everyone was seated.

Roxi had four bottles of champagne open, yet soon was popping more corks, her guests obviously liked the fancy, dry French bubbly.

There was a lengthy welcome speech, in four or five languages, by a member of the local multilinguistic translator's agency. Roxi kept busy refilling the champagne glasses with more of the pricey, vintage Maison Veuve Clicquot. Then the host, a renowned highly notable gentleman at home in Seattle, Washington, spoke. Pointing out that they are gathering in a city famous for world-class Jazz and Blues, he promised entertainment fitting the location. Everybody cheered as the curtains behind the speaker opened up to a stage with two groups of locally well-known musicians.

To the sounds of smooth Jazz music the food-runners delivered tray-loads of Pate Foie Gras, imported French luxury food, to the service stands near each table.

On Bernd's hand signal, the wait-staff started to serve the plates of goose-liver-pate

Strasbourg style. Roxi holding as many as four orders in both hands, three in the left, one in the right, did five trips delivering the delicious appetizer. She placed the plates, as she had learned, expertly from the right in front of each guest. One couple rejected the appetizers with a: "No goose-liver for us." The woman explained it by saying: "My husband and I are allergic to eating anything goose!" He added: "We raise pet geese on our ranch in Utah. We use goose eggs for breeding, we don't eat anything goose." Roxi asked if she could bring them anything else instead, they thanked her, but were looking forward to the next course. Roxi sent those not needed appetizer back to the kitchen. What she didn't know, the cooks were happy to get those two plates back, one of the other waiters had an accident and dropped several plates.

Done with serving the cold appetizers, Roxi grabbed two bottles of the Louis Jadot Pouilly Fuisse and started pouring the dry white Burgundy. She left the champagne glasses on the table because she knew, her group of connoisseurs was not done with the vintage of this particular dry French bubbly.

As her guests finished their cold appetizer, Roxi cleared the plates, from the left. The food-runners were removing the trays and plates and soon returned with small servings of Tomato Bisque. Roxi kept busy placing tomato soup in front of each guest, trying to serve at the same speed, not slower or faster than any one of the other wait-people nearby. It was Bernd who gave the sign to serve the course, so all were in sync and able to work as a team. Roxi knew quite well "That after all, to serve a large group of people is no race, but a team effort. The goal here being to serve a hundred and fifty VIPs in a timely manner, namely as close to possible, at the same time, at every one of the fifteen tables. Roxi offered each guest a choice either the dry white wine, Pouilly Fuissé, or more of the sparkling wine from the champagne, Veuve Clicquot. By the time Roxi was clearing the soup cups and saucers, another speech was being given by a company engineer. Roxi didn't understand most of it, he spoke in broken English, but it was because of the technical terms which made no sense to her. He explained in detail specifics about Internet Protocols and changing the version so that every leaf on earth and every star in the firmament could have its very own IP address.

The band played Blue Trane, as the warm appetizer course was being served. It consisted of Monterey Spot Prawns, three to a plate, with a small scoop of beans and rice in the center. One of the waitresses of oriental heritage had been able to find wooden chopsticks. Roxi had no idea where she got them from. Many more, not only the Japanese, Chinese, and Korean customers requested chopsticks as well. Lucky enough one of the chefs, being friends with the owners of the Japanese restaurant across the street was able to take care of the latest request. Soon a set of chopsticks was added to every place setting.

Roxi poured more of the dry white Burgundy or Champagne, according to each customer's preference. As the wait-staff cleared the plates from the warm appetizer and the empty prawn shells, another much-applauded speaker, talked about the company's future potentials and plans to expand production in China, India, and Malaysia. The food-runners carried in small plates with wet paper towels, Roxi recognized them as 'oshi buris' warm wet towels handed out in planes, as well as in many Asian restaurants where finger-food is served. A nice gesture as well as an opportunity to cleanse the hands after touching food, like the shrimp course. The lengthy applause, following the latest speaker leaving the stage, was the sign for the kitchen crew.

Soon after, to the sound of Jazz hip-hop, the runners brought covered piping hot plates and placed them on service-stands. Five plates to each tray, four trays on four tray-stands near Roxi's tables. Under the hot metal covers, Black Angus Ribeye steak, topped with garlic butter, garnished with artichoke hearts, and Pommes de Terres farcie. Chill out Jazz hip-hop accompanied Roxi, as she served her two tables. And next, she offered red wine, a young, nevertheless rather expensive Rothschild Chateau Mouton from the Bordeaux region.

As soon as all the main meal plates were cleared, several speeches were given, part of it in English, some in other languages, native to certain groups of international guests. Roxi didn't really listen as she was gathering up, removing, all the no longer needed forks knives and spoons. For one guest who obviously loved his bread, she crumbed his area, removing all the breadcrumbs in front of him with her bread-crumber, just one of many waiter's tools, Roxi wouldn't want to be without. And done with clearing her tables, she provided each guest with a clean plate, small fork, and butter knife, as utensils for the cheese course to come next.

More blues 'Now Is The Time,' was being played, as Roxi placed two large cheese platters in the middle of each table, allowing each guest to pick and choose from a wide variety of local and imported cheeses. It included Swiss, Brie, Parmesano, Gouda, Provolone, Tillamook Monterey Cheese, Camel milk, and Buffalo milk cheese, some cheese from the Balkan, and more imported cheese. It was the hosts' wife who walked around and invited people to try the exotics like Tirolian Grey and Austrian cheese from the Zillertal and the Limburger from Belgium. And the wait staff added fruit baskets to each table as palate cleansers. Roxi refilled all wine and champagne glasses still in use and removed all no longer needed empties.

After another, but shorter speech, Roxi took orders for coffee and poured such too. From here on till the end speech, Jazz and Blues provided the background noise, as people were talking, laughing, conversing in an attempt to communicate across language bars.

It was almost midnight when the final speech ended the party. The company president was thanking all those supporters who had been able to attend the welcome dinner and he promised a successful conference weekend for all.

As all guest had left the banquet room, some were heading to their hotel rooms, others to the nearby bars, Roxi and Bernd stayed to help the break-down-crew. She packed up non-needed wines, to be returned to Triples Hotel cellars. All unopened bottles were listed to be credited against what had been checked out from the cellar. Done, she stacked plates on carts.

Staying busy, people-pleasing, serving on time and the proper way, not an easy job, but Roxi was in her element, while doing what she did best, taking good care of people. Yes, Roxi had forgotten all her worries until Bernd asked her, "Say Roxi how are things going, I haven't seen you since the golf tournament banquet!" And that's when she told him about the day she had and her worries about moving. His "One door closes another opens, and usually it's for the better!" gave her much to think, and all in all, she didn't feel bad, just a little saddened. "Whatever happened, by leaving her old place, shall happen. Would she ever find a place, as good as or better than what she had now? Or what will be in store for her?"

Roxi's eyes were lighting up, and Bernd laughed when Hans found them and handed each of them 2 crisp 100 dollar bills. "That's your share of the extra tip for the excellent service from the host." Roxi smiled and thanked Hans with a big hug. Maybe it was that Hans was actually the one giving Roxi a bear-hug, because, without her, this special event may not have been as smooth going. Needless to say, it was Roxi who had been taking care of the president's table. The top VIPs had been evenly distributed between Bernd and her.

Once all was packed up, supplies belonging to the hotel had to be returned to Triples Hotel, rolled across the street on large kitchen trolleys from the Conference Center back to Triples. Both Bernd and Roxi helped with the return of the hotel's belongings. The team of food-runners and the set-up and break-down crew, appreciated the help. All worked hard to get the hotel's inventory back to Triples Hotel.

Chapter 3
Walking home

After the international banquet at the Conference Center, Bernd had offered to give her a ride home, so did Hans. Roxi thanking both, felt the walk up the hill in the fresh cool night air was just what she needed tonight.

Across the street from her apartment building, she stopped, looked up at the stars, it was a clear night with a sliver of the moon just above. She wondered what her mother would have said about all this. About ten years had passed since her mother died in an accident. Roxi had never met her mother's grandparents, who arrived from Denmark around 1900, but she had heard many stories about Lily, her mother's mother. Behind her the empty lot, that's where she Roxi was born, that's also where her father had died. He was from mainland China. Did he die before, or whilst the wooden structure burned down? Nobody ever cared to check on such. He was just one less Chinese fisherman, at the wrong place at the wrong time, living in a mainly Sicilian neighborhood. Sometime after, when her mother became real close friends with the MacMontry clan, she and her mother moved into the apartment, the one she was kicked out from, was asked to leave within two months.

Roxi's mother, Rosa had talked many times about falling in love with the tall Chinese fisherman. He never talked much, could not read or write in English. Rosa, then a working girl, when business was slow she used to watch him while he mended his nets, at the row. She helped him by reading English papers to him. He understood the language, he spoke it as well. Then one day he traded one of his two fishing boats for the little shack. It was just a tiny house with a view of the bay. It was in disrepair. People said he was stupid to trade a good boat for a shed. He fixed it up, and then he asked Rosa to move in with him. It was a big step up for Rosa to leave the place where she worked, just like her mother, like Lily did before her. Rosa's mother, she was one of the lucky girls from Flora's who had one of the streets named after her. Yes, her mother's name was Lily. No, there was no street in town named Rosa or Roxi yet.

The apartment was home. She had lived much of her life here. Except about seven years after Woodstock, she once left the area for some time. She had been on her own for several years back then. Three short marriages later, she visited her mother and stayed. Ever since, except for a short while, Roxi had been living by herself. She had planned to stay forever at their apartment. "Nothing is forever!" she acknowledged her thoughts. Well knowing, it was only for a short time now, the 'forever.'

The first thing getting home was checking her phone for calls and messages. Then she checked her tablet for email because that's what she used her tablet for. Nothing important not even under Junk-mail, where she was used to discover some interesting mail. Having a glass of tea, chamomile, the usual, she was ready to call it a day. Before slipping under the covers, she stared at the locker in the far left corner of her bedroom closet, the one being there for all these years, Fred's trunk, the one he had asked her to keep safe till he got back. "On moving day it has to go, I may not have the space to keep it," Roxi said, not remembering what was in it. For no reason, she looked at the old box. It had been at least 9 years now, if not longer, that she last saw Fred in person. She walked over, removed all those never used blankets and linens piled up on it over the years, and attempted to open the wooden box. The lid resisted her strength. On a second attempt, using the antique cleaver laying there quite handy on the bookshelf, atop her finished book manuscript, she succeeded. The lid creaked and groaned as she pried it open. And the rust-covered hinges squeaked and squealed, howling for something called grease, any oily substance they had not seen in years.

Not giving up, now she wanted to know the box's contents. Looking at clothing, she reached for one old leather jacket. "A worn biker jacket!" Roxi took it out and laid it on the bed. She was then going through the rest of the contents, all clothing, except an envelope on the bottom. She opened the manila envelope, Fred's military papers. Yes, he had told her about his military record, had impressed her with those his war-stories. Slowly she returned all items to the wooden chest. Last the heavy black leather jacket. As she lifted it up, to get a better look, she noticed a leather bag attached to the inside. As she opened the zipper of the oval-shaped bag, a handgun fell out. An old revolver, the drum still loaded. She looked again, two of the six chambers held empty shells. Not familiar with guns, she was still surprised about its weight. It was all heavy solid metal. In a hurry she put the gun back, not even hiding the same, she simply dropped it into the foot-locker. After tossing the jacket on top, Roxi closed the trunk and pushed it back into its corner. In her mind, she wondered, "How could I have missed the gun, when I looked first into the chest, years ago? It was after everyone was looking for a gun. But is this the gun, the one, or maybe not?"

Yes, a long time ago, several plainclothes detectives from CIA and FBI had asked her about Fred's gun collection. Then there was a detective who offered her a reward. This one was looking for a specific gun which had never been returned to the gun maker in Texas. Somebody else also had visited her, because of her ex-husband Fred. And none of them was telling her why and how come they were asking her, except that it was an ongoing investigation, and they referred to Fred as her deceased former husband.

*****

Roxi slept well, she had worked out the night before, not only serving food but schlepping crates of wine. She was not sore but feeling really good, until the thoughts of having to move out returned, and tinted the otherwise sunny day, into dark, ominous, apocalyptic colors. Roxi started to tidy up her living space. Checking her work clothing, both black skirts had barely been used, the work pants, however, one pair not used since dry cleaning. The other, the pair she wore last night needed attention. Using black coffee and a brush, she removed the unsightly spots from her pants. From her seven white blouses, five were not used, the other two went into the white clothing hamper. Black socks she dropped into the reserved for the colored clothing laundry basket. Her work shoes had no luster; polishing made them shine again. The Night Owl sound alerted her that someone from her friends' circle called, and got Roxi's undivided immediate attention. It was Bernd the waiter. "Listen, my dear, I have a friend who does 'Hauling and Moving' to make a living. He is a good guy, he desperately needs work. Unexpected medical bills are haunting him. Why don't you give him a call? You need some help moving and you need Chris. He is good. Call 3757737 now, he is home, just talked to him. Love you, bye." Roxi couldn't say anything except writing the number down. Yes, it surely couldn't hurt to know what it would cost and if Chris could move her, once she found a place, which she hadn't yet.

Chris came by the same morning. Roxi did find him to be the right guy.

Chris looked at her furniture and any other movables, and he gave her a reasonable price for a move within 30 miles. He left her with a "Miss Roxi, don't worry we can handle this move, just let us know when you have your new address, within half a day we'll get it all moved."

Chris had left, and Roxi checked with the La Casa Restaurant to find out on what days and shifts she was scheduled during the next week. They had her in the coming week on the schedule, for five luncheons, no dinners. "Oh well..." she said, "...at least something..."

Realizing that she had never returned the antique cleaver back into its spot, where it belonged atop the 789 pages of single-spaced typed pages. Based on her diaries, and her mother's diaries, and grandma Lily's notes, the book manuscript waiting to meet a publisher was layered with dust, except where an open space resembled the silhouette of the cleaver was asking to be filled by the multipurpose tool. She put what had been used as a paperweight for so many years back into its resting place. As she had no work lined up for the day, Roxi read her boring emails before enjoying a late breakfast-lunch. After brunch she planned on visiting at least five property management companies, to put in an application, and yes she was sure that she would find a place similar to what she had till now.

The First Market Property Co was nearby, and she was greeted by a friendly gentleman, yes they had rentals available.

Before Roxi could see any of those rentals in prime locations, she had to fill out paperwork. And they needed references, credit reports, personal background info and so much more. It wasn't free. A $40 fee had to be paid. Roxi was assured of hearing back within ten days. She went to two more Property Management, those were $50 each, for the paperwork. And there was no guarantee that they would be able to provide what she needed because her income was insufficient to qualify for any rental in the area. She simply didn't make enough dough. So she lied and said aside from her minimum wage income, she makes a lot of tips. This guy looked like he believed her. However, the older lady at that other place, speaking with a slightly foreign accent, mentioned: "My dear lady! We go by tax returns. Hopefully, they confirm what you tell me." Thus all didn't do much to uplift Roxi. It was not her best day. She stopped. After spending $140 and not wanting to waste more money, she quit. Getting depressed, Roxi had enough, after visiting only three property management offices.

The tourist season had not started, therefore to do some job hunting, to pick up another shift or two, Roxi stopped at two restaurants where she knew the managers. She checked if they had any openings, with no luck. Roxi was fully aware of being in need of more work, her income right now just wasn't cutting it. Having to move was going to be expensive.

Chapter 4
Bob's travel plans

As Roxi returned home, in the late afternoon, a box was sitting outside her door. It was addressed to Bob, her neighbor, the fellow who had decided that he had lived long enough. Roxi took the box inside, not sure what to do with it. Yes, Bob had been her neighbor ever since the day she moved in, he even had helped her move in when she returned to live with her mother. Yes, Bob had lived there for 50 years. He was the first renter at the apartment building. Twenty-five years ago when she moved in he said his rent was $250 and yes Bob also took care of the plants upfront, he watered them daily.

Bob had been a salesman for many years. He had accumulated a portfolio of just over 200.000 dollars in stocks by the time he retired about 15 years ago. He was frugal, yet the savings didn't last. Roxi thought Bob was referring to something different when she had visited with him a couple of months earlier. It was that she had been given a couple of bottles of fine wines, and as Roxi had given up drinking alcohol, she gave them to him.

Bob insisted on Roxi's company as he consumed some wine and talked about his life. He had never been married. Bob had a brother with whom he didn't talk, somewhere in Arizona. Bob was telling her that he is at the end of his savings, has just enough money left for a couple more months of food and rent. At this time he announced to her that he made travel plans and is going to move to a better place, a place he can afford, where everything is plenty and no cash needed. No, Roxi didn't take Bob's talk serious, she blamed his talk on the wine consumption.

Ten days ago, when she came home from her lunch shift, Bob's corpse was being loaded into a white van. Two gentlemen asked her questions about Bob, and yes they were sure he was poisoned, the question was: "Who did it? Or did he do it himself!" The answer to her question: "How did he die?" was "He swallowed a large amount of rat poison dissolved in some pricey French wine, we found several empty poison packages next to the wine bottles on the floor!" Roxi's blue eyes were watering, thinking about Bob's leaving without saying good-bye, or did he, yet she didn't listen? And as she knew that soon it shall be moving time for her, Roxi started to take inventory of what to keep, and what to donate for a good cause.

Then her phone's unmistakably revving racecar ring, another fare. It was a couple in need of a ride, from their vacation rental, on David Ave to the Hot Sulfur Baths and Institute. No! Not the same day but the next day, leaving at 9 a.m. from their rental and getting before sunset to the Institute. They had never before been on the Cabrillo Highway but heard much about it. They were willing to pay extra, if sightseeing and frequent photo-stops along the route could be included. This was just up Roxi's alley, she gladly accepted and offered unparalleled driving and tour guide expertise.

Chapter 5
The printer's fax capabilities

A phone-message from the First Market Property Co asked her to fax them a copy of her driver's license. Well, yes, after all, she had this new printer fax machine, it printed, it worked, so she decided to send a fax to the nice gentleman at the property management company. She knew what she was doing.

First, she put the driver's license face down onto the glass, then she pushed copy, and it printed out a sharp good looking copy. Roxi pressed fax, and nothing happened, she waited and tried again, this time the screen showed a number pad. She put in the First Market Property Co.'s phone number, nothing happened. She tried again this time she added the area code, nada, nothing happened. After two more attempts, she found the setup instructions and the printer manufacturers' support number. She called, and a friendly voice answered: "Thank you for calling TP, this is Ben, how may I help you?" Roxi explained her problems, and lucky enough, Ben was willing to do the trouble-shooting. Yes, the fax had power, the fax was connected by a cable to the laptop. Ben asked, "How many connections are plugged into the back of your fax machine?" Roxi's answer, "Two." made Ben ask: What are those cables?" Roxi expertly explained, "The first one is the power cord, the other is plugged in a hole, which shows an icon looking like a cactus." Ben's "And the phone-line?" had Roxi asking, "What phone line?" Here Ben explained that she needed to connect the all-in-one-printer-fax to a landline, using a phone cord plugged into the back of her phone."

When Roxi said, "But it prints fine without a phone line." Ben trying to be very polite, asked: "What kind of phone do you use?" Proudly Roxi said, "The next to the latest smartphone, an iPhone." "Is this the only phone?" he asked. Her "Yes!" Got her a "Sorry Miss Roxi, you got the wrong printer, the one they sold you in the store, doesn't work with an iPhone. If you need to have a fax, I highly recommend that you take it back to the store, and get something different matching your needs." Hanging up with a disappointed "Thank you, bye, Ben." She had no idea that on the other end Ben was laughing as he wrote down on his incident report ID: 10 T the technical analyzing description for "IDIOT" and as explanation: "...unfit to have a fax machine."

As she had more time on hand, Roxi went to her favorite grocery store and asked them for some boxes, yes the young man who always helped her, loaded her VW bus up with folded boxes. He had a phone like hers, busy chatting, he mentioned sending his local girlfriend everyday pictures, and also right from his phone pictures to his parents at home in Guatemala.

Roxi quizzed him, how is it done. He did a show and tell for her "Yes, it is so easy, just take a picture with the iPhone, then click on 'send by mail' or by 'messages' and press the button. Done!" She returned with a load of boxes, and as she stored them, she realized that living on the street and sleeping in her car shall not leave much space for those boxes. Sitting down, she took a picture of her driver's license, clicked on the arrow, then a click on the mail icon, she found the email address of the First Market Property gentleman, it was right there on his business card, clicked send and swoosh it went. Roxi felt good, was proud of herself. After checking her phone for messages one more time, and the tablet for new emails, she turned both off.

Looking forward to her trip down south, she went to bed. In her dreams, she recalled much of the beauty and the craziness of the late 70s along the Redwood Coast.

Chapter 6
Going south

The next day after an egg and toast breakfast, she went and picked up her fare from their rental on David Ave. She had to laugh, as in order to get there, she had to stop, at a stop sign, at the Lily Street intersection. It was a couple from Denmark, Claus and Freja, their hometown, Copenhagen. After introducing herself, Roxi did introduce them to Mathilda, her 1980s Volkswagen Bus. They loved it, aside of plenty of space, the view, windows all around and a sunroof. Helping Roxi with loading two suitcases and carry-on-luggage into the VW, Claus repeated "Yes, we are in no hurry. The reservation at the Institute includes a week-long International conference about the man-made effects of Global Climate Changes, it starts tomorrow, and check-in is after 3, in the afternoon."

Roxi stopped at one of the Spanish era Cathedrals, and again at a Mission, designed by Spanish explorers and missionaries and build with the sweat and blood of the local native tribe. After seeing some of those old, very old gravesites, Roxi made a small detour to show the rock formation where the stones for the Mission buildings were quarried by the local tribesmen.

She explained to Freja and Claus, that what we know as the Cabrillo Highway, the famous Hwy 1, runs along the Pacific coastline from the Baja, namely Cabo San Lucas, at the 0 km marker, all the way to the top of the Olympic Peninsula, and further into Canada, as Canada 1. Roxi promised her two new friends, a grand tour, simply because, they Freja and Claus, had hit it off the moment they met. All three were of the same age-group, 50 - 60 years young, happy healthy-looking people, equally tall, about 170 cm, give or take one or two cm.

Aside from everything else, the box with sodas and a variety of snacks was inviting, but most of all, riding in an oldie, such as Mathilda was making it a fun tour from the outset. The VW's radio had stopped working a long time ago, thus allowed them to talk and listen, and there was no GPS. Roxi didn't need one, she knew where she was heading, and there was no onboard internet either.

On their way, driving south, Roxi stopped at famous landmarks. They walked down to China cove. Here they took pictures with their smartphones, Roxi did the same with her iPhone too. And after spending some time visiting tide pools they drove on. An hour later they stopped at Soberanes point. As the usual morning fog dissipated, Claus opened the sunroof. Roxi encouraged Freja to stand on the seat, and look out the roof, except while driving, and to obey the seatbelt laws. Here they got out and climbed up the hill to take in the spectacular colors of the cliffs below and the blue Pacific Ocean waters. Roxi had brought along a booklet with pictures and descriptions of the local plants, the

California flora. She gave it to Freja, who had fun matching plants along the path with pictures in the booklet. There were the California Buckeye, Sticky Snakeroot, Giant Mountain Dandelions, Silver Hairgrass, Sierra Onions, White Alder, Dog Fennel, Pacific Madrone, Coastal Sagebrush, Wildoats, and a large variety of thistle plants.

Back in the VW bus driving south, Claus and Freja enjoyed listening to Roxi's working the clutch, her switching gears. They loved not only how smooth it rode, but as well Mathilda's most pleasant real air conditioning. Using windows and the sunroof allowed for fresh air from outside to circulate. Roxi did admit that nowadays most cars have it, but from the homes in the local area, very few have air-conditioning. "People living along the coast, rely on Mother Nature and the local moderate climate."

A few miles further, opposite from what was once an important harbor for shipping materials to San Francisco after the Big One, the 1906 earthquake, Roxi took a detour and showed them the Canyon where way back then, workers had built their homes along a creek, strong and sturdy buildings from old redwoods. Here lived the men and women who were mining lime and cutting redwoods to be shipped out. Turning to Freja, Roxi explained: "Lately many of those homes are vacation homes, owned by investors out of the area and many from out of state." Returning downhill to Highway 1 at the end of the canyon road, pointing at the large field with little signs left she let her friends know: "This here was once a large buzzing harbor!"

Heading south, over several bridges spanning over deep canyons, they stayed close to the Pacific on their right, with mountainous terrain to their left. For a stretch of many miles, they counted few trees but lots of brush and rocks on either side of the road. Then the highway led into a valley. Where before next to the ocean they had a light breeze of salty ocean air, entering the valley through Redwood tree groves, it felt much warmer, no wind, a different climate. Here, nestled between the redwoods at the Redwoods Inn, they stopped for a bathroom break. Claus and Freja liked the rustic cabin look and the location so much that they stayed for sandwiches and coffee. They had chosen to sit outdoors next to the river. Roxi couldn't resist talking about her past. She told them stories from way back, from when she hitchhiked, up and down the highway, and shared what hippie life really was about for her. Roxi talked about arriving here at the Inn one night, having no money, asking if she could get some bread, any leftovers to eat. George, who was running the place asked her: "Can you work?" When she answered "Yes" George said, "Sit yourself down girl, order whatever you want!" As she was eating her meal, and she was hungry, hadn't eaten all day, George brought her a time card, asked her to put a name on it, any name. Then he pointed at the time card rack next to the bar saying: "Tomorrow you show up, sign in on your time card, work as much as you want, we have plenty to do. Done working you sign out. When you had enough and need money give the time card to the bartender and he will pay you, for the time worked." There were some tears in Roxi's eyes when she reflected back on those bygone days, "I got paid in cash. In those days they had live music. A band the Abalone Stompers and saxophonist by the name of Jackie Coon were my favorites, not only as musicians but as people, I shall never forget. Good people, real good, generous people, most caring people." Freja asked: "So you stayed at the motel?"

"No we had a couple of Teepees, remember before we got here, the big meadow, that's where we had our commune, our camp!" Nodding her head Roxi added, "Time has changed, the Inn has changed, nowadays people need a real name, a social security card, an ID, background check, and much more to get hired. Back then, they hired people who wanted to work and put them to work. Yes, it was a much different time."

Claus asked: "I noticed cell phone coverage to be spotty at best, down here, am I right?" Roxi nodded her head: "You are right; it's practically non-existent, except for those who use satellite connections."

Driving on, passing the State Park and Lodge, Roxi turned right and headed downhill, in low gear, and past several Estates. Arriving at a small parking area, they departed for a short walk through trees onto the sandy beach. Roxi mentioned that movies had been made here. Freja wondered, "What's the story behind the purple sand here?" Roxi knowledgeable "...many minerals, as well as quartz and garnets, cause the color. Some of my friends used to come here, to get the sand and used it to glaze pottery and ceramics."

Freja wanted to take a handful of the sand home with her. Roxi went back to her VW bus and got a small water bottle, which she emptied and handed to Freja. After taking some pictures while talking about the cold water temperatures, and the very dangerous rip tides, and currents, it was time to get back onto the road south.

Next, another short stop was to show off the Phoenix statue. Roxi told some stories about the neighborhood, including Henry Miller's place and the nearby unbelievable view from the ridgetop on the mountains in front of them.

Driving a few more miles south, and having the gate combination, Roxi slowly in first gear drove up a curvy mountain road. The first mile was a paved two-lane street, and the rest was a one-lane dirt road. It took the VW at 10 miles per hours, nearly half an hour to the top of the mountain ridge. Here Roxi parked in a turnout next to the fire trail, offered snacks and sodas. She did ask both Freja and Claud to stand on the seat bench and take in the view towards the backcountry on one side, and then turn back to see the Pacific in the distance. From up there it truly felt like being above the clouds while watching fog rolling in, far below. They next went for a short stroll, kicking up dust as they walked along the path. Roxi pointed out the Coastal Redwood groves below, and warned both, "...don't touch the tall bushes on the left and right of the fire trail..., ...they look like berry bushes, however that's poison oak, a very unfriendly plant..."

Back in the VW bus, sitting there in the clouds, sharing a can of Grab & Go potato chips, Freja talked about her work in the publishing industry, and how unreal some writing is, just like sitting atop this very mountain range. She pointed at a lonely big rock, sitting by itself on the long narrow hilltop, a stone's throw from them, stating, "...nobody knows how it got here..., ...but there it is." Roxi listened real closely as Freja mentioned her role as an agent working with several European publishing houses, as they watched Claus standing on the seat, out of the sunroof opening, taking pictures, lots of pictures. Claus commented at the blue skies above, then looking down through patches of fog clouds, onto the distant Pacific Ocean, "...pinching myself I ask, is this real?"

Yes, Roxi liked those two at first sight. Claus and Freja, both professors, had never been to the Central Coast. Both talked about the Climate

Change research in Europe, and they definitely did enjoy nature. Roxi knew she would never see her latest friends again, so she did her best to give them an idea of the California Coast, the land where she grew up, and as she knew it. The couple listened to Roxi's explaining in her own words, the wonders of nature, and the beauty of the coastal area. They also heard her voice saying she would love to see Denmark, never been to Europe, but had dreamed about being there, as a child, while reading about the old country and being told that on her mother's side, her family immigrated from Denmark.

Returning down to the highway, slowly in 1st gear, making several stops, it took nearly an hour. Not enough, after a visit in the clouds, atop the ridge, back at the highway Roxi stopped at the next curve, above a famous cove. They walked down a beaten path, over a bridge, and into a man-made tunnel, coming out the other side facing a natural harbor and the ocean. Roxi explained the reasons why the tunnel was built and what the harbor had been used for over the years. She didn't leave out drug smuggling and what have you! She also did mention the Roosevelt home, behind them up on the hill, but did not suggest to walk up there. Before hiking up the hill to the highway above, she did talk about caves, and that there is one just about a stone's throw to the north, with hand paintings, most likely a ceremonial place for natives, from way back at some time long ago.

On the trip south, Roxi told her new Danish friends much about her living and working on the south coast and in the Redwoods during the late 70s. Recalling those days, true it was sometimes not easy. However, she wouldn't have wanted to have missed any of it, because it was so different. People were nice, the "Make Love Not War!" wasn't an empty politician speech, it was a lifestyle, it was a bond between all of them, her and the many-many friends. "There was no bus line, and the traffic was light, however everybody respected hitchhikers, and if you had space in the back of your pickup, or a spare seat in your sedan, you gave people a free ride!" And Freja smiling said, "...back then we didn't have to pay for the trip, see Claus we arrived a few years too late?"

It was getting late when she finally delivered her fare at the Institute. Freja pressed an envelope in Roxi's hand, and Claus said goodbye with a big hug and a kiss on her cheek. Roxi felt elated, filled with joy because she had given them all she had to give when it comes to being a tour guide and storyteller. She took it easy on her ride back. Roxi watched the sunset from a turnout near the lighthouse. It was a beautiful day. She had to have a picture of Mother Nature's painting the sun setting over the Pacific. Her iPhone's black screen was not what she wanted. Disappointed about the expensive non-working camera saying "Stupid thing, damn technology" and she was ready to drive home. Before putting Mathilda in gear, she opened the envelope Freja gave her. Aside from a generous tip, there was a handwritten invitation to stay at one of the couple's homes either Jutland or Copenhagen. Roxi found it to be overly generous from both but knew she couldn't afford it, not even the flight, especially now, as she was looking at most likely living on the street while sleeping in her VW bus. At home, she plugged her smartphone into a power cord, it started charging. Soon the battery showed 1%. Roxi checked for emails, of which there were quite a few, but nothing worth dealing with right there and then.

This night she slept good, and in the morning she stayed in bed longer than usual.

Chapter 7
The La Casa

After breakfast, looking at her calendar, Roxi realized that it was an on-call night, for a dinner shift at the Sassy Station & Bar. She liked the idea of making some money. However, the Sassy Station & Bar meant drunks, drug dealers, and who knew, who else. The thought of getting to wait on Mr.Ventura and Steve was giving her the chills.

Roxi cleaned up her place, took a number of boxes into the bedroom, and packed up clothing she hadn't worn for at least five years, she knew which ones, as that was when she had gained some extra weight around her midsection and never lost. Those older cloth were nowadays too tight. There was a noise at her front door, then a knock-knock. She went and opened the door. It was the Steve guy, the one who had put her on the street in the first place.

"Hey sexy Roxy, how are things going?" he asked smiling at her and acting like he was visiting a good friend. When she didn't answer, he added: "Found a place already?"

Seeing her shaking her head, he mentioned, "If you are really nice to Steve, I get you some extra time, a week, two weeks, maybe four weeks." And the way he was looking her over was speaking for itself. Roxi tried to be diplomatic, yet she answered: "Thank you for your offer, let's talk about such another time. Not today. I let you know."

As this Steve jerk was getting closer and closer, his arm around her shoulder and soon on her back, than her butt, she took a step back. Roxi moving away from him, said, "I have some friends invited, they are supposed to be here any minute!" and added "Sorry but I need you to leave!"

Steve did leave, yet Roxi wasn't feeling okay at all. What was she supposed to do, next time, any time he returned? She knew he would be back. Roxi walked over to Fred's trunk, to the chest, where she knew the gun was hidden. Fred's revolver, thinking to get it and put it someplace she could reach the gun, like the drawer of her bedside table. Steve may want to get her onto the bed. Or if he doesn't, she could entice him to join her on the bed. Then crying rape, bang-bang, and Steve shall be going to hell, where he belongs. Roxi just couldn't help it, she hated Steve, she wished him dead, but no, she was not going to get her hands dirty by killing Steve.

The money-money song from her smartphone saved the day. Roxy was called in, to work at a dinner party, at the La Casa Restaurant. Lucky for her, as such took her mind off anything but pleasing her guest and giving excellent service because that's what loved to do. She did call the Sassy Station & Bar, as she was on call, and yes she was not needed tonight. This way she didn't have to lie, telling them she is sick, because she preferred working at the La Casa restaurant any day or night.

*****

Roxi arrived at The La Casa, one of the older buildings in town, once owned by a family, and run by a matriarch by the name of Hattie, who had made herself a name throwing the most lavish parties in California Alta. After Hattie's death, so the story goes, as she never left the building, Hattie's ghost had been spotted not only in what used to be her bedroom but in other parts of the over two-hundred-year-old, two-story building.

Roxi entered through the kitchen back door. She could feel hectic. The place was busy, not with customers. It was the staff preparing for a busy night, a full house. She was greeted by the Chef, "Look our Roxi is here, Bernd will be happy!" And she felt good by all the smiles she got from the cooks and dishwashers alike. Walking into the front of the house, several of the waiters came to greet her, and she noticed she had been missed. True enough, she hadn't had a shift here for several weeks now. The hostess was busy trying to make sure that she had enough tables for all the reservations, while putting calls on hold, and as needed she asked people to arrive at the late seating namely 9 o'clock. Yet she, Marlissa, stopped doing what she was doing and gave Roxi a big hug, her "I heard about you losing your apartment up on the hill, sorry about it, how is the house-hunting going?" Such didn't do much for Roxi, yet when Marlissa said, "If you need a place to shower, to store a few items, I have a small place, but I have no problem to share what I have with you!" This, however, put tears in Roxi's eyes, because she knew that Marlissa was living in a really tiny studio with very limited space.

*****

Bernd, the same Swiss waiter Roxi had worked with on many occasions, had his home base and five shifts a week doing dinners at the famous La Casa. Not having the staff to cover all reservations, Bernd was put in charge to find a partner to work with, just to take care of this small dinner-party of 17 in Hattie's Room. Yes, if push came to shove, Bernd could handle a party of 17 by himself. However, those people where international guests invited by the head of an investment company and CEO of a Technology Valley start-up. Aside from the large sum of money, the huge price tag, for the small party, they were a very important group of people, and therefore without question Bernd needed a second person. It didn't take him more than a minute to decide on getting Roxi, because of her being a professional wait-person and she used to work with him, hand in hand, at various big events throughout town. Another reason was, that Bernd wanted to help Roxi to get a fulltime job. He felt sorry, knowing that she was working four jobs or more to make a living but was not able to get any benefits, as she worked too few hours, at any one of those places to qualify for medical, dental, or vacation pay as he had. It was Bernd who had talked to the manager, had talked to the Chef de Cuisine and had brought up Roxi's name several times. They all agreed that she is one of the best when it comes to taking care of customers. Earlier he asked the Chef: "Marti, please tell me, why haven't we hired this Roxi yet? She is good. Everybody likes her." The Chef's answer was, "Okay, I hear you...,I agree."

*****

Marlissa pointed Roxi upstairs to where Bernd was busy setting the table. Roxi helped him covering the extra-long table. They had to allow for plenty of space, for silverware and glasses. When Bernd asked: "How is house-hunting going?" She told him about the $140 spent on applications. When she mentioned the last rental agency, the older lady, Bernd interrupted her: "Remember Lisa, the young waitress with two little girls, the one living in her car?" Roxi's "Yes?" was followed by Bernd's "This lady if it's the same, she was able to get Lisa of the street and into housing within no time at all." With "Your words in God's ears." Roxi got the place plates, large ornamental inlaid silver-platters. One for each guest, following Bernd, who made sure that each chair was in the right position. Next, as Bernd folded extra fancy fan-fold-napkins, she started to gather up the needed silverware. To do so, she used a banquet sheet, with annotations by Bernd, he had handed her:

Cold appetizer
Royal Persian Caviar from the Caspian Sea, with Melba Toast
appetizer fork and knife
Krimsekt
***

Salad
Hearts of Palm with French dressing
salad fork and knife
Chardonnay, La Côte des Blancs, Louis Latour

***

Warm appetizer
Abalone Puffs, in the Gallatin's Style named after a famous restaurant owner who used to have a restaurant at Bixby Bridge, Big Sur
fish fork and knife
Chardonnay, La Côte des Blancs, Louis Latour

***

Soup
Mock Turtle soup "Lady Curzon Style"
soup spoon
***

Fish Course 1
Coquille Saint Jacques
fish fork
Chardonnay, La Côte des Blancs, Louis Latour

***

Fish Course 2

Fillet of Sole filleted and served table-side
fish fork and knife
Chardonnay, La Côte des Blancs, Louis
Latour

***

Palate Cleanser 1
Strawberry sorbet
dessert spoon
***

Main Course 1 beef
Chateaubriand cut and served table-side
meat fork and knife
Bordeaux, Chateau Margaux Pavillon Rouge
***

Main Course 2 venison
Saddle of venison served table-side
meat fork and knife
Burgundy, Gevrey Chambertin 1er Cru Les
Champeaux

***

Main Course 3 lamb
Rack of lamb carved and served table-side
meat fork and knife
Mateus Rose Portuguese
***

Palate Cleanser 2
Raspberry sorbet
dessert spoon
***

Cheese
Danish Blue Cheese
small fork butter knife
Choice of Champagne Dom Perignon
or
Burgundy
***

Dessert
Banana Foster
dessert fork and spoon
Choice of Champagne
or
Dessert Wine, Chateau d'Yquem Sauternes
Blend

***

Mocca
Cognac, Louis XIII

Still having 2 hours till the party's arrival, Bernd proudly let her know that since he worked at La Casa more than 30 hours a week, they had put him on medical insurance. "Hurrah that's the best news I have heard in a long time!" Roxi congratulated him saying "I haven't had insurance since a long-long time, can't get enough hours to be full time, glad I am getting what I get on part-time jobs, to pay rent, to eat, put gas in my car, and once a month I may treat myself to a movie," and "if I get sick, I don't want to think about such to happen."

When Bernd asked "What about the PickMeUp, the Car-Ride-Share-On-Call deal?" he was surprised about her answer "It hasn't been worth doing these past few months. But, Bernd I had a couple of unbelievable good fares lately, like the other day down to the Hot Baths & Sulfur Institute. Beautiful people, good money too. " Bernd laughed, "You are quite something, I am happy for you!" Looking at her, nodding his head, "You are a very good person!" After placing the silverware, ten sets of knives and forks, soup spoons and dessert spoons in the correct order, and finally the dessert spoon and fork above the place settings, Bernd added his Fan-Fold-Napkins. The Champagne, white wine, and red wine glasses for each guest came next. Then both, Bernd and Roxi spent a good deal of time in making sure those glasses were properly lined up. At about the same time, they got done, the lady from the flower-shop delivered two low flower arrangements. And once the candle holders and the salt and pepper shakers were added, the table was ready.

They still needed a full silver-reset-plate, all the wines, plenty of ice, coffee, cream and sugar, the small Mocca service, the flambé set, butter and rum, and two decanter setups. Yes, all in all, a small party but nevertheless a big production, but that's what these extravagant multi-course dinners are all about. As Roxi downstairs in the waiters' area, across from the kitchen, was getting her breadbaskets ready, Marti, the Chef de Cuisine came over to her. Looking Roxi in the eyes, he asked her: "What does it take to get you to quit the Sassy Station & Bar?" "Another gig that pays the rent," Roxi answered.

"Look Roxi I will talk to the manager and the owners, somehow I will get you a full-time job here before long. Everybody likes you. We want you here."

Roxi: "Chef, so what do you want me to do while I am waiting to get here enough hours? I have to pay the bills."

Marti answered: "Roxi please, please quit the Sassy Station & Bar, there are drug dealings going on. None of us here at the La Casa wants you to get drawn into it when the shit hits the fan." Convinced and knowing that he was right, Roxi stuttered "Okay, yes, yeah, Chef, I promise, I quit the Bar!" without really knowing why. However, thinking of this jerk Steve and his uncle were enough reason to quit the Sassy Station & Bar. The Chef's words were on her mind as she watched Bernd decanting 4 bottles of some rather outlandish expensive, old Bordeaux wine, to let it breathe and be ready to be served.

As the dinner party arrived and the guests sat down, Roxi poured Krimsekt, sparkling wine from the Krim area in Russia. And she started with the foreign national official who had been pointed out by the host with the words "...take good care of his Excellency..."

Bernd brought two tray-loads of covered appetizer plates up from the kitchen. After a welcome speech by the host, Bernd and Roxi served elegant garnished plates with a small portion of the finest Persian Caviar on top of Melba toast, and a teaspoon size order of chopped hard-boiled egg and onions. Roxi poured more of the Krimsekt, Bernd added baskets filled with bread and several dishes with butter. While the guest enjoyed their hors d'oeuvres, Bernd went and brought up the next course, the salad course. Then both cleared the caviar appetizer plates and replaced them with the small order of Hearts of Palm on a salad leaf with a sprinkle of French dressing. With it they poured more Krimsekt or French Chardonnay, as per each guest's choice. After clearing the salad plates, they allowed a 10-minute break, before serving the Abalone Puffs, brought up by two chefs. Those were served atop a bed of sauce remoulade, two per person, garnished with Italian parsley.

Marti the Chef the Cuisine gave the group his spiel about the origin of those Abalone Puffs, and the famous gastronome who had introduced them first to Central California. Marti also commented on the surprise courses still to come, the Lady Curzon, Coquille St Jacques, Sole in white wine sauce, three different meat courses, cheese, and the Banana Foster flambé. With this, he the tall-white-hat-chef returned to take care of the backlog of orders in the main kitchen.

Both Roxi and Bernd brought each a tray with small soup-cups filled with hot Lady Curzon, up to Hattie's Room. Because of the egg-white-lid, there was no worry about the soups, heavily laden with Sherry, getting cold. While the guests savored the soup, Bernd set up a filleting station, with enough space for two rechauds to keep a large silver platter warm. He also allowed for space for a sauce bowl or two. Next, to it, he wheeled the electric plate-warming-cabinet, stocked with 51 dinner plates. As Roxi cleared the soup cups and saucers, Bernd carried a large tray up the steps from the kitchen, surrounded by a whiff of wine and spices. The tray he carried above his shoulder was loaded to the max with small plates. On them, seashells, displaying scallops in a creamy white wine sauce, topped with breadcrumbs and cheese, the source for the pleasant cloud of appetizing and delicate aroma. They served the Coquille St Jacques course, again Roxi started with his Excellency. Then poured more of the Chardonnay, except one couple who liked to stick with the Russian sparkling wine.

As Roxi and Bernd cleared the Coquille plates, one chef brought up two sauce bowls with white wine caper sauce, followed by a second cook carrying a large silver platter with five large pan-fried Dover-Soles. After presenting the silver tray, garnished with lemon and parsley to the party, he placed the platter onto the two rechauds; the filleting station set up by Bernd. The other Chef went and got a small container with rice and a scooping-tool. One filet of sole, one scoop of rice, a slice of lemons, a garnish of parsley each order, one plate after the other, looking like a copy of the first plated by the young cook, served by Roxi, as Bernd refilled the wine glasses.

After the fish course plates were cleared. Time for a 10-minute break, followed by Strawberry Sorbets to cleanse the palate. Another chef brought up a cutting board, carving knife and fork, he whispered something into Roxi's ear and left. Roxi followed him downstairs into the kitchen and brought a covered container with asparagus spears, one with Pommes Dauphine, and a bowl with French steak sauce.

As Bernd cleared the sorbet dishes, Roxi fetched the large silver-platter with 3 thick tenderloin steaks, garnished with sliced beets, and kept it warm on the two rechauds. After a short explanation out of the hearing range of their group of guests, Bernd agreed with the change of service, because they were swamped in the kitchen and none of the cooks was able to provide the table-side help, as planned, including the showing and carving the meat courses. Bernd's "No problem! You carve! I serve it!" wasn't a question but a confirmation that he knew she can do it, will do it right. And nobody will ever know that the kitchen crew, had just dropped the ball on them.

Bernd went around and poured a small amount of the decanted Bordeaux wine. Then he was ready to serve the meat dish as soon as plated by Roxi. He watched Roxi presenting the show-platter with the whole fillets of beef, then after placing the large silver-platter on the rechauds, she removed one of the filets to the cutting board. She perfectly sliced the steak and plated two thin slices of tender filet of beef, asparagus spears, and Pommes Dauphine. To complete the artistic display, she added two slices of beetroot and topped those each with a dab of spicy French steak sauce. The next plate just like the first one, one more and another, until she was done with creating seventeen small main-course servings on piping hot plates. By the time she finished the last plate, Bernd had already served all but one. This last one she served to the last person not yet devouring his tender Black Angus meat slices. And Bernd did another round with the red-wine-decanter.

Once they cleared the beef-main-course plates, Bernd served more of the red wine, Roxi went around the table, and reset silver-ware as needed, here a knife there a fork, just to make sure that everyone had the right utensils to attack the next course.

Then Roxi went and got a bowl with wild mushrooms, and a special red-wine-sauce, and a covered container with Pommes Croquette. Soon after, one of the cooks arrived with a large platter holding a saddle of venison, garnished with mushrooms and cranberries. After presenting the show platter, he sat it on the rechauds and returned down to the kitchen. All eyes were on Roxi, who expertly carved the meat from the bone, first one side, then the second side. Nothing but the bones and garnishing left on the hotel-silver-platter. Having both filet-look-alike long pieces of lean venison next to each other on the cutting board, she sliced through both at the same time, each one 17 slices. And she plated like she did before 17 equal plates, on each now at first a spoon full of dark red-wine-sauce, then placed two pieces of venison on the bed of sauce, added mushrooms on top, and garnished the plate with two Pommes Croquette, and a sprinkling of cranberries. And as each plate was created, Bernd served the most delicate New Zealand Cervana venison main-course. Yes, it took nearly ten minutes for carving and serving, but that's what the guest enjoyed so much, they didn't come to spend several hundreds of dollars per person, just to eat and run. Those people were here to tease the senses, to relish food, to taste some of the best wines the cellars had to offer, and get expert service at one of the highest rated places in town.

It was close to half an hour later that the 3rd meat course was carved and served. Here again small servings, of the boneless rack of lamb, tender roasted with garlic, thyme, salt and pepper, and rosemary, served with mint sauce, surrounded by green string beans and Pommes Anna. To provide a fresh taste, a little sparkle, a rose, the Portuguese Mateus Rose was poured now, and it was refreshing, complementing the flavors of the lamb.

As they cleared the plates, they also cleared all, but the-still-in-use white-wine, red-wine and champagne glasses before they brought up and served the raspberry sorbet palate cleanser. Clean champagne and wine glasses indicated that there was more to come. Bernd served plates with crumbles of Danish Blue Cheese placed on oversized croutons, surrounded by a small handful of seedless grapes.

Roxi having a bottle of very special Burgundy in one hand and a bottle of Dom Perignon Champagne in the other, filled up the glasses according to each guest's request. It happened that almost everyone preferred the Dom Perignon, only one lady wanted to try the Burgundy style Pinot Noir from South Africa. She passed her glass around and soon everyone wanted to try a sip of the obviously, unexpected for Roxi, most outstanding best-tasting Pinot ever tasted by anyone in this group of wealthy wine-lovers and connoisseurs.

The group was chatting, joking, laughing, and having the best of times. Give or take 45 more minutes until dessert time. Bernd and Roxi had tossed coins as to who does the flambé. He didn't mind she won, he had seen her doing table-side-service many times, and he was proudly working with her, because of her style, being level-headed, her know-how and ability to handle people, food and drinks, as well as any table-side request. Roxi got 17 bananas, a small container with cinnamon, and two sticks of butter, sugar and a bucket of real vanilla ice cream from the kitchen. Bernd had raided the bar and was back with a bottle of French Cointreau and a bottle of Dark Rum. While Bernd went to get plates for the dessert, Roxi split each banana in the middle lengthwise, but she left the fruit in the peel. Ready for the final show, all eyes were on Roxi. She lit the gas burner, and warmed up the flambé pan, doing so, she poured sugar into the middle of the pan, a good amount, topped it with butter, and let the sugar melt, allowing it to caramelize. A splash of orange liquor for flavor, staying back as the alcohol burned off, she then added half bananas, without the peel, on top of the caramel sauce, a sprinkle of cinnamon on the bananas, a splash of rum, standing back as the flames were reaching for the ceiling. That's when Bernd started to scoop out vanilla ice cream. As the flames got lower, Roxi put one-half banana on one side, the other half on the other side of the ice-cream scoops. She poured and spooned the caramel sauce on top and Bernd served it, still hot, here and there a flickering blue flame as the plates arrived at the table. And Roxi did it two more times, showing off her skills, and when someone asked her if she had done this before, she honestly answered: "Yes, at a food show, 4 hours without a bathroom break, for about 200 plus people."

And as more Champagne was poured, there were more requests for the unique South African wine.

They offered Mocca and they poured several glasses of ancient very expensive cognac, but most people stayed with the Champagne.

It was past midnight when his Excellency complimented Roxi for the exquisite execution of the dinner service, including carving and flambé. He then went to Bernd gave him a business card and offered him a job at the best place in Dubai. Turning around, he found some folded up papers, which he pressed in Roxi's hand, and she slipped it in her pocket, as others were in line shaking her hand, complimenting her for the job done. The VIP dinner party made their way down the steps, out the door and boarded their waiting limousines. Ned, the manager, came upstairs and let both Bernd and Roxi know about the rave reviews from each and every one of the party guest as they had passed by him, in leaving.

They broke down the tables of party setup, and Bernd asked her about her training as a wait-person in table-side service. She promised him to tell her story, the one about washing dishes so she could eat, being chosen to help in the kitchen to prepare food, and finally put on the floor by this Sepp, a German restaurant professional with seven years of hotel school, apprentices as waiter-cook-manager, and world traveler, to be his assistant. "But it's a long story, and we may not have time for it tonight!" Bernd agreed "I understand!" Recalling how she started out at the Mountain Resort when this German fellow, this Sepp told her: "Young lady if you are willing to listen to my instructions and show up for work, I promise to make a world-class waitress out of you." Back then, yes, she was not only desperate but also willing and agreed.

"The result was amazing…, …"

After cleaning up and putting the room back to what it usually looked, Roxi remembered those two pieces of colorful paper. She hadn't seen any of these before. His Excellency had given her 2 Euro banknotes each saying five-hundred. Showing them to Bernd, he wondered who got the better deal, he got a job offer, and she got a thousand Euro as tip. Roxi insisted that he keeps one of those banknotes, still wondering where she may be able to cash it in, "...do I have to go to Europe to get my money's worth?" Jokingly Bernd said, if I get a job in Dubai, I fly you in, every time we have a VIP banquet, and both laughed. Done, Bernd went to meet some friends in a bar downtown, and Roxi went home.

She had left her phone at home, checking she found that she had ignored two calls. "Too bad, can't be helped. Too late, too early to call back." She said to herself. After all, it was already 2 o'clock in the morning. This night Roxi slept deep and good, the workout at La Casa was just what she needed, to let her forget any negative thoughts, especially the one of feeling worthless, useless, no good. It was that work, the customers, the coworkers, especially Bernd had given her what money can't buy, a value of self-worth, the knowing her being wanted, needed, and appreciated as being Roxi.

Chapter 8
Joannie

It was past nine in the morning when she got up. She had some toast and a glass of milk before turning on her laptop. The last time she used it was when she bought this all-in-one printer-fax-copier. She was proud of herself that she was able to connect it all, she put the ink in, following the instructions. Then put the white paper in the paper tray and connected the printer with a cable plugged in at the printer and the laptop, and voila it worked when she printed a webpage. Well then the other day, she found out that it doesn't fax. The printer did everything else, copy and print! "Should I return it because of the fax malfunction?" Roxi wondered. But then since she knew how to send pictures with her smartphone, she answered herself, "Who needs a fax, when you have an iPhone?" She laughed, "I don't."

She was then checking for email on her tablet, again nothing worth her time. So turned back to the laptop to search, to google apartments for rent. And she kept on searching, next a red screen came up, in big letters it said: YOUR MICROSOFT LICENSE HAS EXPIRED, you must call 1 866 666 666, or your network will be shut down. Reaching for her phone, a knock on the door changed Roxi's plans to call Microsoft. Some cursing words on her tongue, she shut the laptop down, the fast way by pressing the power button and counting to ten. Attending to the knocking at her door, what a surprise, it was her Steve, the jerk. He had misunderstood what she said the other day, taking it as an invitation. Here he was handing her a gift of chocolate and some edible whatever. Taking it as a peace symbol, Roxi was trying to be nice. He talked about her being missed last night by everyone at the Sassy Station & Bar.

She looked, then opened the gift-wrapped package to see what kind of nourishment, may be hidden. He had brought her, according to the label an Edible Condom with French Ticklers, much disgusted she threw it at him. He was good at catching. Steve started to explain; it all went through both of her ears. She didn't need to hear his "Sorry if this offends you!" "I just wanted you to laugh!" "Honey it's a joke!" "It's not what you think!" "I'm..." as he moved closer. Roxi was trying to come up with a non-combative way to get rid of him and find a peaceful solution to the aggressive and threatening situation. Her laying down and let him do what he came to do, it was an option, she didn't fancy at all. Another knock-knock on her front-door gave her a much-needed break from listening to Steve Godzilla's sweet talk, who was now using every nice word he could find to bolster his coming on to her.

Roxi escaped his touching hands, she opened the door, and if it had been the undertaker asking her to come along on a coach ride to hell, it couldn't have been any worse. As Roxie, holding the door open, was frozen in place, Joannie, Roxi's 3rd ex-husband, with big smiles was throwing the arms around her. Joannie was hugging her like such was going out of style. After the immediate shock, trying not to freak out, while being surprised, angry, and extremely upset, Roxi got a grip on herself and used the situation to her advantage.

She turned around facing Steve and with a loud voice yelled at him: "Mr. Godzilla, you may zip your pants now, unless you want to get it on with Joannie, my ex-husband, 3rd husband to be more precise. Oh yeah, don't forget to take those condoms with you. We don't use them!" Not at all being happy about Joannie showing up, however, seeing her as the lesser of two evils, Roxi shoved the speechless Steve out the door. Joannie's shouting "Don't you bastard dare touch my ex-wife, my sexy Roxi, or I send some of my friends to break your arm, both arms, you hear me. If that doesn't help, I may drown you myself!" got Steve's attention. And if not, as he got down the steps and to his car, it was blocked in. Inches behind his car was parked a moving truck. And in front of his car the Bentley Cabriolet with license plates well known to him.

Steve realized after several failed attempts that he couldn't use his car until one of those others either the truck or the exotic Bentley moved. He was swallowing on his own ego, holding off with any action against those two, the butch and her girlfriend, because he comprehended the facts "Yes, that was the daughter, the wild one, of the family, those people, the owners of the water rights throughout the valley, the same, who own a large junk of the coastal frontage too." Steve clearly recalled, way back when he was a child, what his parents told him about those people, that they are scrupulous and don't shy away from any action against anyone who dares to offend their way of actions and lifestyles.

While Steve was undecided as to walk back to his office, wait or call a taxi, Joannie was having a ball. She was telling her friend Roxi all about the safari trip, about the long neck Giraffe she shot, then a Wildebeest, as well as a Warthog. "Can you imagine when I put a second bullet into the pig's head, I slipped in its poop, fell and damaged my titti."

"What?' Roxi asked

"Somehow, one of my breast implants went flat!"

"How?"

"I don't know, but I had paid to shoot two more animals, an Elephant, and a Rhino, big bucks, yet with the sagging bag on one side and the DDD size on the other I looked lop-sided,!"

"So, who fixed it?"

"I called family friends in Tel Aviv; their son is a doctor. He recommended Dr. Walder in Vienna. So I took a private-jet from Joh'burg the same night and by getting my tits done, I did lose out on hunting those big animals I had paid for."

"But everything is okay with you?" Roxi asked, somehow she did care for this crazy wild woman, the one she was once married to, for less than six months. And Joannie showed her both breasts. Roxi complimented her by acknowledging that whoever did those implants, did an excellent job. Joannie's "Well they are what they are, yours are as nice but natural. I was always jealous of yours, you know!"

Roxi couldn't wait much longer, therefore asked: "What brought you this way?" "Listen, darling, I have those two strong big blokes, Afrikaners, rugby players, and they aren't impressed by my girlfriends, to them they are lightweights, too childish, too young, inexperienced, they need someone mature, a real woman. It pays real good. You get to travel with them for a month in the US, Canada, and Australia. Let's go. I know you can use the money!" Roxi could feel her heartbeat increasing. The word money was getting to her.

Yes, she needed the money. Then again she relived in her mind the days, the nights, the weeks she was with Joannie. It had started with being at a party at Joannie's five-bedroom condo. Then they went to her boat. After a week in Acapulco, they flew back to Vegas, where she married Joannie. Then both left to join a party in the Bahamas. She remembered, it was a tough job, the being shown around by Joannie and handed by her to some of those fellows, who just wanted to get to know what Joannie's latest girl-toy was like. They both left, and on the flight she got some rest, only to wake up at the airport in Dubai. But this was only the beginning of party-life and more. Roxie had and did always do, what Joannie wanted her to do. Roxi was nothing but a slave to Joannie's never-ending new ideas, and her seemingly endless number of high flying, affluent, international male and female friends. Roxi was not allowed much of a choice if any. Then one day, she broke free of it, she had it, had enough, she wanted her own life back. Yes, and she put in for divorce while Joannie was somewhere in Europe on a Greek island, giving a party for her friends. It took Roxi a few minutes before she told Joannie: "Well I am not interested, I am doing okay, I have a good life, some stress but I can handle it. I am sure you can find someone else who will do her thing of entertaining your South African friends."

"Really, you refuse my generous offer?"

"It's not your offer. It's the lifestyle, mine is so different now. By the way, thanks for coming by, I have to go to work soon."

"If you are this way, okay, bye babe..." and Joannie without saying one more word got ready to go, but a voice from her watch, stopped her "Joannie, 10 minutes to your manicure appointment, traffic is light, leave now!" Joannie laughed. I nearly forgot, I have to go now.

As Joannie drove down the street, she saw the Steve fellow, at the street corner, Joannie couldn't help it, but honked her horn and gave him the middle finger.

*****

Meanwhile, in her apartment, Roxi lying face down on her bed was crying hysterically, beating with her fists on the pillows. Having had to face two of her biggest nightmares within the hour, she had her nervous breakdown. Freaking out, Roxi thought she had enough problems. She didn't need this Steve guy coming on awfully strong to her, and not her ex-husband to try to set her up with some big Afrikaner rugby player blokes. Finally, after resting exhausted, she crawled off the bed, pried the lid to Fred's locker open and took out the revolver, which she put under her mattress, knowing sooner or later she will have to use it, because she was not going to make it easy for Steve, if he dared to come back, and she had little doubt that he would be back.

Chapter 9
The Place

Getting back to normal, after a freaking out morning, Roxi remembered that she had to call Microsoft. She turned the laptop on to get the number. Back on the internet, the screen with the urgent, call Microsoft message, was gone. Not having the phone number, she didn't call. Unbeknown to her Microsoft does not alarm end-users with pop-up-screens threatening to shut down the network. It was a scam. After having a tuna sandwich for lunch, she packed her VW bus with boxes filled with old clothes, ready to be donated. On her way Roxi stopped by the Sassy Station & Bar and talked with Dan, the manager. Yes, she could have called, but for some reason, because she had been hired in person by him, she liked the idea of quitting in person. Yes, she planned to let them know that she had been promised a full-time job at the La Casa and therefore will no longer be available to be scheduled. The manager, a charming Scottish fellow, was disappointed when she told him: "Dan, thank you for hiring me and giving me shifts when I couldn't find a job anyplace. However, I have landed a full-time gig and therefore, will no longer be available to work for you!" Dan, was shaking his head, then confessed: "Darling, you are the best, but what am I going to tell Mr.Ventura about your leaving us?" Roxi's "Why would he care?" Got answered with a "You didn't know, he owns the property, the Sassy Station & Bar and the liquor license all outright free and clear!" "Wow! Really? No! I didn't know!" A very surprised Roxi was thanking the manager, and wishing him all the best. In leaving Roxi was happy. Knowing that Steve's uncle was the new owner at the Sassy bar and nightclub, made it much easier for her to break up all connections and sever all ties with the Sassy Station & Bar. She just couldn't stand the guy, this Mr.Ventura. Thinking of Steve she felt like throwing up.

The drive to what used to be China-town took about 30 minutes, as she arrived there, she stared in disbelief at the number of people sleeping in tents, or just on the ground along the street, the same she remembered as a vibrant place of nightlife, back in the good old times. Walking down the street, looking everywhere for Nicole, she couldn't find her friend. Entering a place that was once a bar and restaurant but now run by a welfare organization, she found a fellow who looked like he belonged to the establishment. Roxi asked him, "I have some extra clothing in my car. Do you think your organization is interested in clothing at all? A donation of good used clothing."

"Yes, so many of our friends here have very little, and clothing is always in demand," he answered. Roxi went back where she had parked and drove to the building with the carved wooden sign saying The Place. Here she started to unload her VW bus. Soon some more hands were helping her to carry the boxes inside. As she was getting ready to leave the man she had talked to, he asked, "Mam do you needed a donation slip for your taxes." Her answer was no, yet then she recalled why she was there in the first place "Do you know a Nicole Schreiber, blond, mid 40s, she lost her apartment, lived in her car. Then her car broke down, and last I heard was that she is living on the street, here in your neighborhood."

He nodded his head "That's about everybody's story, can't afford the rent, die or living on the street!" and with an "I am Richard, a volunteer here, I cook lunch and sometimes dinner for my homeless friends. There was a Nicole, she had a really hard time fitting in. Yes, she came last month. Not sure if it's the same, but that Nicole left with a bunch of guys driving a motorhome, with big plans to get out of the state."

Richard nodded his head again, "...the only another Nicole is a woman in her 80s, looking forward to the afterlife, ready to die any day now, she was sleeping on an old discarded mattress on the sidewalk, till we got her a tent on her eighty-first birthday, last month."

The news visibly shook Roxi. What Richard didn't know was that there was a time in her life, when she ran away. It was the time she got married in Las Vegas. Coming back a few months later she was caught selling dope while visiting Sacramento. It got her some hard time. It wasn't that time but another time when running off with some guys, she got arrested for a felony, did time, had a baby behind bars. She gave the little one up for adoption at birth. Yes, the felony charges were later dropped, and all that showed on her record now was a misdemeanor offense. Well to be true, Roxi had to admit she had been in trouble with the law more than once. Yes, and every time it was because of a man, some men.

Richard offered her a cup of black coffee, asked her to sit down, and he talked with her for quite some time. He was letting her know, "...those people, those called homeless, have a home just like everybody, it's this planet, and it's our earth. They all have the same sun, the same air, the same wind, the same rain, like everyone. However they have less access to water, food, housing than more financially well off people, because of disabilities, unable to earn the money needed in today's world and no helping hands or connections. Most of my friends are loners, lost souls." He ended by saying: "If you give me a phone number or address, I shall let you know when anyone sees or hears about the latest whereabouts of your Nicole." Roxi wrote her name on a piece of paper he handed her, she added her phone number too, saying: "That's my phone number, I recently got my 60-day notice, after living at one and the same place for 25 years. So I don't have a place to live, but I have a PO Box, where I get my mail. Luckily I just got a full-time job, still not enough to qualify for a 3000 dollar apartment, because that would require that I make 9 Grand a month. Well, I am a waitress. I am happy if I make 3 Grand working four jobs." Roxi realized by sharing with Richard her fears, her problems, it took the edge off, somehow she felt less pain, was not anymore as stressed out. She left not without asking Richard for a hug, thanking him for listening and his help.

Driving home, Roxi stopped by the Post Office, nothing but some advertisements in her mailbox. As she got to her apartment, she was exhausted. Roxi had an irrationally and uncontrollable day filled with madness, plenty of excitement too. The perfect recipe to freaking out. Some extra rest sounded like a good plan. Therefore she went to bed early.

Chapter 10
Full time and benefits

This most beautiful day was not only sunny bright, with a smidgen of salty air in the light breeze. It was also the beginning of Roxi's full-time employment. Well, she didn't know this yet, for what she had in front of her, were those five luncheon shifts at the La Casa. However, she had Marti's promise to get her more hours at La Casa, provided she dropped the Sassy Station & Bar and nightclub work, she had done so, had quit. Roxi had faith in Marti, a good man, the Head Chef at La Casa, if he said so, it was going to happen. She knew it.

The days went by fast. Roxi had been working her five luncheon shifts at the La Casa Restaurant. They were good shifts. Roxi did prefer the dinner shifts, the money was better, as most parties tipped 20% plus and the average ticket per guest was always above $100. She was much surprised because even at lunch she took on average over $100 home in tips. At the last lunch shift that week, as she was picking up orders in the kitchen, Marti complimented Roxi: "Not only do you walk and carry trays as good as any waiter, you talk like an experienced international trained waitress, the kind we need here." Not sure why Marti said so. However it became clear to Roxi when Ned the manager complimented her for being able to pronounce menu items the like of Perigueux, Mousseline, Kromeskies, Cassolettes, Escargot, Epinard, and Madeira, expertly, not silly like some servers did, trying to make their customers laugh, which at times didn't bring the expected laughter but complains about the wait-persons ignorance. Roxi knew too well not to advertise rack of lamb as saddle of a poor little lamb. The venison was not Bambi's mother. Duck Confit was not Donald Duck twice-backed and preserved in lard.

And the escargot salad should never be called gardener's-revenge-at-the-slugs. She had learned such a long time ago, when this Sepp, that German waiter trained her and made her carry trays, his way. He made her carry five plates, three in the left hand and resting on her arm, 2 in the right hand. Back then, she thought that was brutal and that he didn't like her. If not so, he enjoyed it, the torturing poor Roxi. Now it paid off. She was accepted at the La Casa and highly respected as a professional waitress, and part of an international team of servers at the best French restaurant in town.

Roxi knew the menu, and how to pronounce the often strange sounding words on the bill of fare. She was reading up and learning about the wine selections, and was able to explain all food items in detail, to anyone. She had spent years refining her abilities to sell by practicing sales gestures and phrases. Roxi knew it was critical not to hustle customers like a used-car salesperson. But equally important was to show enthusiasm and sincere belief in the kitchen's ability to produce the best food in town and her serving and presenting the food the only way, the proper way, and pouring and decanting wines in style and always at the right, appropriate temperature. Roxi knew there was nothing wrong with using persuasive words to paint a positive picture in the guests' minds. There was nothing wrong with the practice to make a diner's mouth water by being descriptive. Her teacher, this Sepp, had been emphasizing that it is an excellent sales tactic to create an irresistible craving for what the server is trying to sell to the guest. Roxi had experienced over and over that successful sales-tactics result in the desired mind-change of an undecided customer. Sepp had told her over and over "Once the customer wants that which you have to sell, then you know that you did your job. That is the point at which you cease talking unless you want to kill your sale." Roxi knew "...it's my job to bring what the customer wants." Quite often, her customers did not know that they wanted something until she told them what they wanted. Once the guests ordered what she wanted them to have, it built up the guest-check, sold what the chef wanted to sell, pleased the manager, and made the customers happy. Roxy never endorsed or promoted items she wasn't sure that they were the best money could buy. During these five days, of working lunch at La Casa, Roxi worked one day with

Ralph, a British waiter, and she got to meet Allye, a French waitress and Hilda from Germany. The waiting on tables at the La Casa for lunch was such that downstairs each waitperson had a section and worked by herself. Upstairs they ran two-men-teams, one person being the front-waiter and stayed on the floor, always keeping in contact with the guests in the station, while the other as back-waiter did the running down to the kitchen to get the orders. Roxi did know from experience that at times they worked as so-called three-men-teams having one front-waiter, one cocktail-wine-waiter, and one back-waiter. The idea behind it all was to make sure that customers did get the quality of service as expected in a 5 star French Restaurant.

Marti was right. Ned took her aside before leaving, after the fifth lunch shift, and said: "We want you to be full time working for us here at the La Casa." Roxi with an open mouth was listening, not sure what to say. "Starting as soon as the week after next week, that's by the end of this month, you are scheduled for three split shifts. The same the week after." Ned added. All surprised, Roxi still hadn't been able to say a word.

"Does this work for you, Roxi?" Ned asked.

"Yes, yes, oh that's so cool!" she was tearing, as with this offer, a dream was coming true. Ned confirmed her hopes and dreams: "From then on, I shall make sure you have every week at least enough hours to qualify for our rather generous benefits program."

"Thank you, thank you!" was all she could say. Without her noticing, Marti had joined them. The Chef de Cuisine started to praise Ned for making up his mind and getting Roxi to be a full-time member of the La Casa crew. The fact of having one good paying full-time job, having medical, sick leave and vacation benefits made her feel rich. Roxi was very excited emotionally, ready to freak out, happy-as-a-lark, never mind the grimmer realities of life, namely having to move and having no place to move to.

Chapter 11
Going north

Leaving work, arriving at her VW bus, her iPhone in hand she felt the vibrations, curious she looked, and as the phone's display showed Hot Baths & Sulfur Institute, she answered. It was Claus who called. The Danish professor. He inquired if they could rent her car and her as the driver for a day. "Roxi, the conference is over, only one more photo op tomorrow. Freja would love to see you. We have reservations at the Airport Hotel in San Jose. Therefore if you are free, we would greatly appreciate it if we could twist your arm and bribe the Roxi bus-tour-company to provide us with limousine services."

"When?" Roxi asked.

"The day after tomorrow," Claus said.

"May I pick you up at 9 a.m.?" Roxi inquired.

"Excellent, yes, we shall be ready and waiting," he said. Roxi had no gigs at any of her workplaces in the next few days. Thus the fare from the Hot Sulfur Bath & Institute to the Technology Valley was a most welcome gig. Best of all she was going to see her friends again, Freja and Claus. Roxi loved the two, just because they were real nice down to earth people. Yes, in general, the driving didn't make her rich but kept her busy and added an extra paycheck to her low bank balance every so often. However at times she hit the jackpot, like meeting her Danish friends Freja and Claus.

Recalling Freja's words, talking about her professional life, her working with publishers, Roxi took the very old cleaver of the dusty pile of papers, memories from the hippie days returning fast. The rustic hand-forged cleaver showed its age. It was made from one solid piece of steel a long time ago. Roxi had found it in the river near the Redwoods Inn where she worked cleaning rooms. As she and her friends lived the hippie life under the redwoods, this cleaver had come very handy and seen many uses, as hatchet, knife, chopper, and ax. A leftover from a different time, its usefulness tested, by cutting and slicing food, chopping wood for the fireplace, and carving tree-trunks. It hadn't been sharpened for many years but still had a nice edge. She had gotten a lot of good uses from this cleaver. To defend herself against an attacker wasn't one of them. No, the cleaver was a tool to survive, cut food, cut kindling, not to hurt anyone. She looked for another spot to place the cleaver back on the bookshelf, it just didn't fit. The cleaver looked out of place, lost without the manuscripts. Therefore she took it over into the kitchen, thinking about using it as a chopping tool, the way it was thought to be used.

Back at the manuscript, after dusting it, carefully she fit the unbound pages into a leather pouch. She had bought the expensive-looking bag to hold her writings, while attempting to peddle her book, to any interested party. She had been longing to get those hundreds of pages published. The book she wrote on for more than 12 years. However, all those willing to publish Roxi's works, they wanted money, asked her to pay large sums for editing, printing, advertising, and who knows what. She never had the money for it. Roxi went downstairs and put her life's work, the story of Lily, into the VW bus, right under the driver seat, next to the wheel-break-block.

The next day she had Mathilda serviced, filled up the tank, washed it, and was ready for the day-trip.

*****

It was cold in the mid-fifties (Fahrenheit) as she left on her trip down south. It took her only 3 hours to get to the Institute. She arrived ½ hour early than planned. However, Claus and Freja were ready and waiting. As a surprise and added sight-seeing, Roxi drove further south, as far as Jade Beach. Parking at the side of the road, they all got out. Freja and Claus followed Roxi climbing over a low fence, they, Roxi first, then Freja and Claus last, crossed the meadow, the grass was still green and tall, except the well-trodden path displaying dirt, and here and there a rock. Coming to a stop atop the cliff, they enjoyed the light Pacific Ocean breeze. In front of them, a surprisingly good set of steps cut into the soft-rock-formation allowed to walk down to the beach, littered with many sizes of rocks, not just any stone, Big Sur jade. After taking some pictures and putting a small flat rock into Freja's and one in Claus' hand as souvenirs, they took the steps up, and crossed the meadow, returning to the waiting Mathilda. Freja commented on the smell, the Ocean, the salty air, the temperature much like at the Baltic Sea, and asked Claus "Do you feel it, the humidity is much higher here than at home?"

Roxi turned her car around, and they were heading north on the curvy two-lane road, called Coast Highway 1. "How many corners on this famous highway?" Claus asked. Laughing, Roxi answered, "Too many curves and smoothly rounded bends to keep count of, all we can do is drive careful..." Soon they stopped at a State Park, to take more pictures. This time Roxi had an iPhone charging cable and the cigarette lighter connector with USB ports on hand, just in case. Here they spent a little over an hour, which included admiring several lime kilns from an anno 1800 lime-calcining operation. They walked into a forest of old-growth redwoods, and took pictures while admiring a 90 plus foot waterfall with the clearest cold mineral-rich water. As there was no wind, the temperature felt much warmer than 62 degrees. The air was clean, the sky blue, no clouds overhead.

And Mathilda took them further north, where they passed another State Park entrance. Shortly after, Roxi pulled into a turnout overlooking the blue waters below. Roxi knew she was in Condor country. She offered some snacks and sodas, as she talked about those Condors. Roxi wasn't sure if she could show off one of those birds, the ones with up to 10 feet wingspan. However, she knew that they were at a popular condor-watching location. And Roxi explained: "...the California condor is the largest flying bird in North America and can be found in forests and rocky areas of Alta California, Arizona, Utah, and California Sur." It was Claus who pointed out towards the Pacific, not even a mile away, spouts, a group of whales was blowing air and water as they came up, close to shore. Seeing parts of their large dark bodies surfacing, Freja counted three. Looking up above them through the open sunroof, there it was, a big bird, a condor, Roxi pointed up. Claus and Freja got on the seat bench and through the open roof took many pictures. Added to the first one, they had three more Condor sightings.

In the sun, it was warm; the light breeze of cold ocean air was most welcome. Heading further north, driving at the edge of the world, to the right the tall coastal mountains, to the left the Pacific. Roxi noticed her two friends were impressed by Mother Nature and scenery. At several areas where the mountains had lately been sliding into the Ocean, the bare-mountain-formation, once hidden by a layer of topsoil, was exposed.

They made a bathroom stop at a building looking much like an oversized water-tank, nestled into a canyon, housing a gallery and coffee shop. After admiring the gardens, the paintings and wood carvings, and sculptures, a cup of coffee and a sandwich were in order. Looking out over the Ocean, a small fog formation was ever so slowly finding its way to the coast. Talking about the importance of fog, Roxi mentioned, "It absence of heaving rain outside the rainy season, a lot of native plants depend on the fog for nourishment."

Back in the car, heading north, Freja remembered having read Big Sur and the Oranges of Hieronymus Bosch by Henry Miller, as they stopped at the Henry Miller Library. Claus talked about books by Fritz Perls; he had read many years ago.

Next Roxi was pointing at a complex up on the hillside. Like every place this one had its very own specific story attached to it as well. Roxi told them about these nice folks, the previous owners, who went and borrowed 300 thousand dollars, in the late 70s. A short term loan to make some improvements to their land, the campground, restaurant, and motel. When the note became due, a year later, the bank didn't extend the credit but foreclosed. A prominent investment company in Los Angeles acquired the property and made plans to bulldoze the old redwood buildings to make way for lasting luxurious concrete structures. When it came to rebuilding, the local contractors poured concrete, following the available plans. The buildings' walls were all up, the roof was added, when the principal investor visited the property. To his surprise, everything was ass-backward, the kitchen on the ocean side, and the restaurant looking at the hills behind it. Once he found out that whoever copied the plans had done a horizontal mirror flip, it was too late to start over. Some people believe "...it deserved them right..." and "...the ghosts ghosted the plans to get even..."

From here through the valley they passed by another State Park. Leaving the redwoods, it was a short drive, to a spot where the highway followed close to the Pacific, and the old Coastal Route was winding up into the mountains. The latter was the road Roxi chose, a mixed pavement and dirt road. Arriving at the mountain top, they looked back down over grazing land, part of a large cattle ranch, before driving downhill into the woods. Around many bends and between old redwoods, then along a river, they passed fern-laden hillsides. And more old redwood groves, soon arriving at an early settlement, before driving uphill again. The climate changed several times, and there was no wind, it was cool in the woods, warm in open areas. A different world, like the time stood still, paradise style. Roxi called it "God's Country!"

The Old Coast road rejoined the highway at one of the spectacular highway bridges. Here pointing at a turnout on the ocean side, Roxi let her friends know "This very spot used to be a famous restaurant in the 1950s." And she followed up with the story about the four Pilipino waiters playing cards, one night. Then because one felt cheated, he killed his three friends to get his money back. Soon after, the restaurant was pushed over the embankment into the Ocean by a bulldozer.

Heading further north, they went over another equally picture-perfect bridge. Passing Westmere, Roxi told them the story about the house of ill-repute which stood in this location during the days while the road was being built. She revealed that once business slowed down, the madam laid fire to her property and traveled with her girls further up north.

Next at a point where a restaurant was sitting high up on the rocks, allowing an unobstructed view onto Notley's landing and the first bridge down south, Roxi let her friends know the restaurant was built and run by two chefs for many years. They always had a good time during the summer. However, every winter, they were fighting with each other and trying to sell. Back then in 70s, there were no takers for it. As soon as spring changed to summer, they were the best of friends again. "Nowadays it's just another priceless property along this unique coastline."

Passing what's known as highlands, Roxi pointed at a hotel overlooking the Ocean, Roxi told the story about a Swiss family who used to own it in the days she hitchhiked up and down the coast. The old man died. The lady kept it running. She had three young fellows from Texas staying at the hotel, and one of them at breakfast asked her if she ever would want to sell. Naturally, she said: "Yes, if the price is right." "How much?" one man asked. Taking it as a joke, because they didn't look like big spenders, she answered, "Not less than 12 million dollars in cash." Before the weekend was over, she received a 12 million dollar cash offer. That was during a time when homes in the area were going for 50 to 100 thousand dollars. She accepted the offer. The day, the deal closed, nobody in town had a check-writer to write such a sizable check. The escrow officer had to travel to the county seat, 40 miles inland, to get a 12 million dollar check printed.

Passing the old Mission they had visited before on the trip south to the Institute, Roxi told the story about the Native tribe, about a missionary marrying the chief's daughter, just to make it easier to get the rest of the tribe to work and help to get the buildings finished. The same Mission housed the headquarters for all Alta California missions for many years. She shared what Roxi knew from one of the tribe's elders, namely that disease brought in by the Spaniards and alcoholism decimated the local tribe fast. And about the tribe's sacred lands, now all is being lived on by the later arriving Europeans, without paying rent nor showing much respect for the original owners, the tribe.

On the highway heading over the hill, they passed by the cities of the peninsula. As Roxi was talking about sacred land. She told the story about Dick, a devout Christian Scientist, rich developer, and builder. Having the necessary cash, he noticed a beautiful piece of land, near the harbor. Nobody else had ever built there before him, because it was known to be a sacred native burial ground. Dick made plans, bought it, and soon turned it into a small business center on what was known to be for many hundreds of years the cemetery for the local tribe. After enjoying his success for several years, proud of his achievements, having reached a certain fame for his spectacular development, he stepped into a rusty nail. Because being a Christian Scientist and not seeing a doctor, he died from blood poisoning. His wife, now the only heir of the buildings and land, put the property for sale at a bargain price. She sold it within 48 hours and moved away within a week's time, far away, fearing the wrath of those who were buried and resting below her business center.

Pointing at the bay on the left and the rows of old looking rotting away barracks and homes, at the right side, because Freja asked, Roxi gave them a rundown of the history to the once-famous military base and training grounds. "There used to live about 35 thousand plus soldiers on the base. Not counting the officers living in the two adjacent cities, where business was booming all based on the needs of young men, getting ready to fight for the country."

And they headed towards a harbor town recognized from afar by the two large smoke-stacks. On both sides of the road, Claus and Freja admired fields as far as the eye could see, and more fields with what looked like a thistle plant. Roxi answered Freja's question about the agriculture in this area, "These are artichoke fields." Roxi turned into the little town amidst the fields, where she bought three orders of fried artichoke-hearts at a small take-out place. Neither Claus nor Freja had ever eaten artichokes before. They enjoyed the snack.

Roxi was driving by the twin towers of the power plant at the harbor town. She stopped at Jetty Road, for a short walk, a fishy smell was in the air, it was getting windy, clear skies above, whatever fog they had seen before, had all been blown away. Here Roxi told her passengers about her experiences working as a waitress at one of the places, and it was nothing but a hilarious story until the sad part. "It was when I followed the invitation of a nice fellow, some guy who always had lots of money. We got married in Vegas. The marriage lasted nearly a year. By then, I was doing time in prison for selling drugs. He had disappeared. However, he did show up at my apartment one day, about seven or more years ago and left some luggage, a footlocker in my care, only to leave within the hour to unknown whereabouts. He did say he would pick his stuff up, within a week or two. It hasn't happened yet."

Driving further north, half an hour later Roxi left the highway, passing an airport, and onto rural roads with apple orchards as far as the eye could see. The climate had changed, it was warmer, and no wind. She stopped in the middle of a small town, at a meat market. Roxi didn't know that butcher shops in Europe are much like this particular meat market, an unusual sight in California. Anyway, both Freja and Claus were impressed by the quantity and quality of the butcher shop's sausage products, and most of all that all the meats were all apple-wood-smoke-cured. Roxi purchased roast beef sandwiches for all, and got some sodas too. Sitting outdoors on a bench, surrounded by apple trees. They enjoyed their late lunch.

From here driving inland, on a windy road over a pass, they were getting closer to their destination, and they could see in the distance a city. Roxi turned left, and below a mountain famous for being ground zero at the last big local earthquake, she showed her two European friends the picture-book setting of a Swedish community nestled in the woods, in-between and next to waterfalls. As they were sitting on a bench at a redwood table, listening to the wind in the treetops above, the waterfall in front, a variety of birds calling each other, Roxi mentioned "Freja would you know someone who is willing to have a look at my writings. I have spent a lot of time to document my family's life, more exact Lily, my grandmother's affairs, all from my diaries?" Freja's "Where is it, at your home, can you please send it to me?" was answered by Roxi's "Just a moment, and she went to Mathilda, got the pouch with her manuscript and handed it to Freja, with an "If it's no good, and no takers, just send it back."

Within another hour, Roxi delivered her two friends to the Airport Hotel. Asked about the fare, Roxi decided to tell them that it was on her. All because they had treated her so generous last time. "It was a fun trip, not just for you, but myself too, today. See it allowed me to get out and enjoy the day, allowed me to forget the miserable housing situation I am in. But it all is looking up. It's working out, I know it. Yes! I know God willing it is." Claus smiled, thanked her and assured her that he plans to make up for it in Denmark, as soon as she comes over and visits. Here Roxi admitted her situation. Thanking for the most generous invitation, but not being able to purchase an airline ticket, at least until sometime after finding a place to live.

"Having a steady full-time job now, and a good income is already a step in the right direction!" She said, "Once I get all situated and moved, I promise, I start to save for the ticket."

Chapter 12
Ransomware

Driving back home, the radio at full blast, Roxi was humming along. Life was so good, amazing. Soon the thought about feeling guilty, was creeping in. It started to overwhelm her, the "I am feeling good, but do I deserve it?" thinking. So many positive events lately, the blessings in her daily life, she realized that it wasn't all of her own making. It was just happening, for reasons unknown to her.

At home, the first thing she did was check her emails on the tablet. Thirty-some emails from all over the place, VIAGRA advertisements, RUSSIAN women galore, all kinds of pills to buy, investments in whatever form, invitations to donate money, several more of them from various political party candidates, and nothing useful at all. Yes, she clicked on one which offered Easy Money with No Work. It was in a language she couldn't read. She thought it was Chinese, but it could have been Japanese, Korean, or any of these writings. Roxi caught herself cussing at the stupid tablet, questioning its ability to provide useful email, calling it dumb. She was sure that artificial intelligence had been left out when they made this particular computing device. She knew there had to be some good, pleasant, enjoyable email out there with over 3 billion computer users world-wide. Then why did she get only crappy mail?

Opening the laptop, and not too sure why she was turning her laptop on. But soon she googled the words: email, meaningful, tablet, excursions and did one or two more searches. Then the screen turned black, all black. Before long in bold large letters, in red, a text appeared:

YOUR PERSONAL FILES ARE ENCRYPTED BY A XYZ LOCKER, then below in yellow text, she was told that she cannot use her computer, followed by more red text flashing and telling her to get a certain amount of Bitcoins and deposit the same into an account, once done her files shall be released to her within 24 hours. Clicking around, trying to get past the message that some ill-meaning, sick artificial intelligence had allowed some crooked somebody to hijack her computer. Finally, she was giving up. Roxi heard herself saying, "So stupid, I have nothing on the computer, what did they encrypt?" After shaking her head, she turned the laptop off, the way she usually did, holding down the on/off button and counting to 10, and with it temporarily escaped the tyranny of technology.

When she turned it on again, the ransomware notice was still there, filling the screen. 300 Bitcoins? Not sure how much it was, too much for Roxi. Since she had read news about that kind of attack on computers, knowing that city government, state officials, and federal government agencies had been paying those crooks to get their computers back. She wasn't going to deal further with it. Planning to take the useless laptop back to the store where she had bought it, was the only right solution, she could think of. Not to forget to take it along she put the laptop in its sleeve and carried it down to Mathilda. There was plenty of space in the back, and in there, it went, on the floor. She realized that she had left the box, with the empty sodas, in her VW bus too. There were also some unopened bags with snacks still left from the trip. Looking again, she did see an envelope with flowers drawn on it right atop the snacks. Taking it out it was from Freja, a note thanking her for the generous snacks, the most informative tour, the save driving and especially the loving, caring company she had provided. Included was a booklet with five $100 traveler checks, signed ready to be spent. On the cover, it said, "We don't need these dollars anymore, at home we use Kronen and Euro. Hope, you can make good use of the US money, Claus."

Upstairs in her apartment, laying on her bed, extremely surprised, Roxi was freaking out, crying, confused and happy, not knowing what it all meant. As the tears stopped, she got ready to get a good night of rest.

*****

On the day after her road trip, still Roxi hadn't heard anything from either one of those three Property Management offices. She was tempted to invest another couple of 100 dollars in rental applications. After all, she had made more money this past month than ever before in several months. First, what about those $140 she had shelled out previously for those pending rental applications?

First she drove to the computer store. Here she showed her laptop and the ridiculous ransom demand screen to the salesperson. The same, after realizing that she had this computer less than 90 days, decided to help her out. He called a Richard a technician over and showed it to him. Richard explained, "Miss Roxi, I know we can reset it to factory settings, and all your data is gone! Which you say, you don't have! However, because you are a good customer, how about we keep this one." She didn't understand. Richard corrected himself, "...we keep the encrypted laptop, and you get a brand-new laptop." Roxi thought, "That's okay," and she started to understand the technician's plans when Richard said, "I may want to play with it and attempt to break this specific encryption. It's a good training tool for our technician team too. You do not mind if I give you a new laptop, one from an open box?" Her "Yes, sure, that's a good deal, thank you, thank you, that's great, I like the offer..." words meant just such. Roxi was surprised and very happy about the outcome by bringing the laptop back to the store. She promised to come back and sent lots of business to the computer salesman and his techie team. Having a new, non-invaded laptop, looking on the outside just like her old one, but inside still a virgin, not raked-over-coals by some ungodly foreign outfit trying to squeeze money out of poor Roxi, things were going good, the day had started in her favor.

Chapter 13
Property management

To check on the progress in her search, and the availability of apartments for this or next month, Roxi stopped by The First Market Property Co. She entered with great expectations and the highest hopes based on the friendly reception last time and thus changed when she was informed that her credit report was no good, her income insufficient, and her criminal past disqualifying her from becoming a renter in any of the First Market Property rental properties. The gentleman whom she had met last time, was this time much less gentle, especially when he opened the front door for her and asked Roxi to leave with a "Sorry to say Miss, and a Good Day! Under the given circumstances, we are not able to be of any service to you!"

Feeling lousy, having lost all confidence and self-value, because he was right, she had little money. She had a checkered past. Roxi was on her way to the other two rental agencies, and she was not expecting much success whatsoever. The next one was as bad as or worse than the first one. Here she was accused of lying on the application about income, the criminal record, about having a real job, and everything else. Her being freakish in saying, "But I spelled my name right, and my social security number, didn't I?" didn't change anything. Debating in her mind: "Shall I go to the last one?" Beaten enough and having reached the point of feeling worthless, a low point, could she really go any lower? Roxi was unsure in her mind if she should go and see that old witch, the grey-haired woman who had told her before that her income was insufficient. She had less than the littlest of a tiny bit of hope. Saying a fox-hole-prayer, asking for help, Roxi, was ready to turn around and run away. Then with a go-girl-never-mind-the-outcome, it's just an old woman, on her mind, she was willing to face number 3 on her list. To Roxi's utmost surprise, this woman had been waiting for her. She had a to-do-list for Roxi. Her name-tag said, Ellen. The same introduced herself to Roxi by letting her know that she was once a penniless British immigrant, who got quite fortunate herself. However, as a number of her best friends can't qualify for a rental due to their limited income, and the nowadays exuberant rents here in California, Ellen was encouraging the hopeless feeling Roxi, as she kept on talking about her own experiences with finding low-income rentals:

"Yes, I was able to help all, but one of my friends and all those I sponsor, to get a place to live!" Looking Roxi straight in the eyes, "My dear young lady, you must apply to those agencies on this list here at once!" Roxi couldn't say anything when Ellen added: "You need help, filling those applications in, let me help you, no, no charge, and come back anytime." Roxi's blue eyes were filled with tears of happiness, deep down having the feeling that this woman, this Ellen, actually cared and wanted to help her get into government-funded housing. She was talking about going home and do the needed paper-work.

However Ellen insisted for her to sit down at the empty desk near the window and start adding her info to the low-income house program form, next was a rental assistance application, then local subsidized housing and something called section 8 housing. Somehow deep-down Roxi knew that she was on the right path as long as she followed the instruction of that incredible nice grey-haired lady. Done, Ellen checked each form and put a sticky on each. Then she urged Roxi, "Now waste no time. Here on those tacked-on-notes are the addresses. I noticed you have a car, go and hand-deliver those papers yourself today, do it now. Make sure you get the name of the person you hand your application to." Roxi stared at the woman in front of her. Ellen further told her: "Let me know whom you talked to, when, and at which one of these agencies. Here is a notepad. Bring it back with all the names, and if you can their phone-numbers and job-titles, it's important. Do it not later than tomorrow. How about today, come back as soon as you are done?" Ellen's word's "Go now, do what's in front of you, first things first. Miracles happen. Go, get to work!" and a smile sent Roxi on her way. She spent the next hours delivering her applications, Ellen's words were on her mind: "First things first. Miracles happen." Yes, Roxi, was familiar with these sayings, or was she not?

Done! She returned to see Ellen and handed her the notepad with the list of names. She had recorded day and time she saw each representative, his/her phone number and job titles. Yes, Roxi had followed Ellen's instructions without ever questioning her, as to why and what for. Compared to earlier, when she saw an energetic Ellen, this time around, aside from looking very pale, Ellen's hands were shaking, and all in all, she didn't look healthy at all. Ellen noticed the question mark in Roxi's eyes "Don't worry, go now. I have to take my medications. See you soon..."

*****

Returning home, after having a snack of rye-bread and cottage cheese, she decided to go on what she called "Do the laundry trip." The washer and dryer at her apartment building had died in-conveniently just before that Steve bloke took over. After driving around town, where there used to be laundromats, she found one still open for business. The Filipino lady managing the laundry facility offered to do the laundry for her, and for a small fee fold and hang the clothing. All to be ready for pick up the next day. Roxi was happy and gladly accepted to pay for such services. After all, right now she felt rich, hadn't she had an unusually good month, the rides, the wait shifts? When she heard that the Filipino lady was doing the extra work to earn money for her kid's school lunch, books and what have you, Roxi was ready to be generous when tipping at pick up time.

Leaving the laundromat, and getting into her Volkswagen Bus, Roxi felt positive, she was optimistic and anticipated to find an affordable place to live sooner than later.

*****

She had time off, before starting three days of split shift at the La Casa. Yes, she was getting shifts now, getting enough hours to call it full-time work. Feeling rich, by having a booklet full of traveler checks, and cash in her pocket, Roxi went window-shopping for a newer car. She was looking for a modern VW van to sleep in, also usable for her PickMeUp ride shares. That was not an easy task, and those VWs which may have worked for both purposes, like a newer Volkswagen Vanagon, was far above her budget. Never mind that at both the VW dealership as well as a used car lot, the salesmen assured her that she would easily qualify for a loan, as long as she brought a piece of paper stating that she is full time employed, for at least six months, which she wasn't. Listening how little she would get for Mathilda, her much loved Volkswagen Bus, such was another shocking experience. It really hurt her feelings, after all, she had been waltzing the roads with her Mathilda for over 30 years, and they had together traveled more than a quarter-million miles. She had had only once, about ten years ago the engine completely rebuild. Tom, the mechanic, downtown, had been doing all servicing and upkeep for her loved van, for at least a dozen years. He surely knew all about Mathilda's ins and outs. Tom was the one who had given her the 10-pound car-wheel-stop block, the one with the initials M-R. Ever since, she had used it when parked on a hill, where she put it under one of the rear wheels to avoid any possibility of the handbrake not holding and Mathilda rolling away. The same wheel stop block came in handy whenever she was on the open road, going down highway 5, or up highway 99. By placing the ten-pounder on the gas pedal, the VW's engine would go at maximum, equaling cruising-speed of 65 miles and purring steadily down the road, the best and very reliable cruise control option for her Mathilda. She decided to forget about replacing Mathilda and called it "...abandon window-shopping, it's time to retreat."

Only after she got home, after turning her smartphone back on, did she see the messages and phone calls received, two PickMeUp fares, both for short distances, and supporting messages. Too late now. Time on hand, she made friends with her new laptop, connected it to the printer, and all worked. She scanned a picture, and it worked, then she copied a document, thus worked too. Just to see, she tried the fax, it didn't work, and with this result she was sure, it was the stupid printer, attempting to play games with her, and no she was not going to fall for it. Roxi felt in peace with the world. The positive attitude didn't last. First, she dropped her smartphone on the kitchen floor, picking it up, she noticed the crack in the glass. Ready to check for email, her tablet was locked, and whatever she did, she couldn't unlock that device. Next while walking around the apartment, she was wondering why she got kicked out. Yes, she liked the apartment. It wasn't even 1000 square feet. What would that

Mr.Ventura do with a small two-bedroom place? She knew that he lived on a large property, with an elaborate house. She had seen photos of his estate, located on several acres, overlooking the golf course. "Surely he wants it for one of his bimbos." Roxi thought and "I need to move out the sooner, the better, but why doesn't anyone want to rent me a place? Just a small place. I need a roof over my head before the rainy season starts..."

Stocking up on negativity, Roxi was torturing herself, was having a terrible time, and she was wailing, sobbing and weeping while feeding her resentments against all those people un-willing to rent her a place.

Chapter 14
Split shifts

Time had gone by fast. By now she had replaced the broken glass on her iPhone. She had replaced the Android tablet with an iPad mini, and her laptop was working just fine. Still, it didn't fax, but that was okay with her. Roxi had been looking forward to getting started to work her scheduled Tuesday, Wednesday and Thursday 10 to 12-hour shifts. Thus still left her with Friday, Saturday, Sunday, and Monday for additional work and income.

Roxi felt very energetic, happy, grateful, feeling blessed to have a full-time job with benefits. The first day she arrived at 9:30 for her first split-shift at La Casa. This day she worked from 10 a.m. to 3 p.m. luncheons. At lunch, many customers know what they want, and that's what they order. The "May I take your order," write it down, get the drinks and food, serve it and get them the check is typical lunch. However, there are also exceptions, people who want to be pampered and are willing to go all the way when it comes to multi-course meals. She had several tables of the kind who wanted to indulge, nothing but the best was good enough for them. And Roxi was having a field day, doing what she most enjoyed doing, taking good care of her customers.

After lunch Roxi went home and was back by 5:30 p.m. dinner service started at 6 o'clock. This night her last table left at 11:30 p.m. and she was able to go home, just before midnight. At dinner, most customers want to be entertained. Starting with "What may I bring you tonight? How about one of the specials? Do you care for some wine recommendations?" was always a good start, the getting to know what the guests had in mind. Once Roxi knew why her customers were here for dinner, birthday, business meetings, anniversary, or whatever the special moment maybe, she was ready to upsell and recommend the best kitchen, bar, and cellar had to offer. The goal "...to make it a night to remember, a dinner worth talking about for days and weeks to come."

HI (human intelligence) is based on information which includes, all senses, and whatever little information their memory may have stored. Creating new situations worth remembering that was Roxi's job, and that's what she did best, and much enjoyed doing.

The crazy hours didn't bother her but reminded her of the time when she had no money, many years ago. Fresh from jail, let out at 4 in the morning, barefoot trying to avoid the rain, cowering under the roof-overhang at the backdoor of the Mountain Inn, that's where two of the maids found her. They fitted her with some shoes from the lost and found closet. The chef when he arrived fed her but didn't forget to tell her that nothing is free, he needed help washing dishes. That day, she was happy to have something to do. She had some hope to be able to stay in the shed, the one holding the cushions for the outdoor seating arrangements. The chef, after talking with the boss had said: "Provided you do a good job, you can stay in the shed out there, it's dry, and it's just a short time solution." Yes, back in those days, she worked from morning till closing, and she was proud of doing a good job. At least that's what everyone said. Coworkers brought her clothing, the food was plenty and excellent, and she had no time to worry about anything because she was busy, really busy.

It was two months later, with the second paycheck she rented a cabin nearby. Some of the coworkers dropped off a table, a couple of chairs, and a bed. She had her own place. Two months later, she started helping out in the kitchen. The chef wasn't going easy on her. However, she learned, learned, made plenty of mistakes, and that's how she learned. After nearly a year at the Mountain Inn, having learned much about food preparation, soups, sauces, fish, meat and desserts, it was this Sepp fellow, the German guy, he needed an excellent reliable crew to work the floor, doing table-side service and he chose her to become an example for all. Yes, Roxi didn't mind working many hours, because she knew to be busy doing what's in front, leaves no time for crazy thoughts. Mister Sepp he used to say: "Who rests too much, will rust too much too!"

Yes, on her first split-shift day at La Casa, the customers, all of them were very appreciative of her service, her being attentive but not overbearing. Aside from this, the coworkers expressed their feelings of being happy to have her finally full-time as part of the La Casa family. If given a choice, Roxi would have wanted to work dinner shifts only. The idea of spending five out of seven nights in the most pleasant surroundings of a fine restaurant was for her the dream job. Roxi knew that at times one needs to have worked those floors of low bottom places or seedy bars, the fast food, and the overrun coffee shops, in order to appreciate the five-star ambiance, the best of food and cellars, aside from the precious benefits. Working in restaurants some nights are better than others. However, in general, working dinners are less stressful than luncheons. Diners have more time, the customers aren't ready to run but like to sit to enjoy.

True all Homo sapiens are part of some amusing species. Human intelligence is on occasion cross-wired, short-circuited, unpredictable, illogical, based on cognitive features, and at times egocentric high levels of motivation and self-worth. At dinner time it's very entertaining to watch the games they play.

The second day on split-shift she arrived at 10 a.m., did the setup, started serving at 11:30 a.m. and her last lunch-table left just past 3 p.m.! Home for only about 2 hours she was back before 6 p.m. This night Roxi was part of a two-men-team, their station, upstairs the salon. Roxi worked the front, Ricardo an Italian waiter, worked the back, schlepping all the food up as needed, clearing tables, and allowing Roxi time to schmoose with the customers. Their dinner crowd was made up of so-called upscale gentlemen and their women, one table with politicians, several wannabe screen stars, and some nouveau riche business leaders in a celebrating mood. Plenty of cocktails, only the best from the wine-cellar. One table, trying to impress each other and their waitress, by ordering the only bottle of a 55-year-old Red wine, a $9000 bottle. They were wondering what will happen if the waitress drops the bottle. One of those rich guys, all 4 were in the mortgage and insurance business, asked the question, "...who is liable for the loss, if she messes up, the restaurant or the waitress, does she have insurance?" Another was offering "I bet you that old girl doesn't know how to serve such good wine!" Roxi, heard some of the conversation, one ear in the other out. She presented the Merlot, a Petrus Pomerol, very carefully, with the bottle resting in a wine basket, to the host of the four-top. She moved slowly mindful and guarded, as not to disturb any of the sediments. He approved and remarked, "...sorry to hear that you have only one of those; it's an excellent wine if you had more, I would buy them all..." Roxi used a service trolley, with a decanter, and a candle, here very carefully Roxi removed all the foil from the bottle's neck. Then very nicely, like she had done many times before, she opened her waiter's knife and screwed the corkscrew into the cork, all the way, to make sure not to break the old cork, or let it separate into pieces. The dark color of the cork gave her an idea about how to remove it. Whatever happened, Roxi didn't want any cork crumbles in the wine. And slowly, very slowly using little pressure on the corkscrew lever, then more, until the cork moved, first just a millimeter, another millimeter, then a centimeter, and yes it was in one piece, as the old cork came out. This cork she presented to the host on a small plate. He looked at it, smelling the cork's aroma. He was nodding his head, before passing the cork around the table, while Roxi at the service trolley, lit the candle. Holding the decanter in an angle with one hand, with the other hand she lifted the basket with the old Bordeaux. She held the bottleneck just above the flame, thus allowed her to see the small stream of aged red wine slowly flowing into the decanter. And carefully she poured the high priced wine, stopping just short of allowing any of the bottle's sediments to be transferred into the decanter. Finished she offered a small taste to the host, who after smelling, swirling and tasting approved of his purchase and Roxi poured each of the four a small amount of the Merlot. On the host's request, she put the decanter on the table. Everyone commented on the just perfect color, body, and nose, of the Merlot. Roxi left the service trolley with the near-empty wine bottle next to the four top. As they had their food coming, one of the guests asked for the red wine sediments, so he could use them on his bread instead of butter. She got him a little bowl and poured the sediments for him.

This night almost all her customers were drinking too much, and none of them was very impressive in such a state. Yet some thought they were actually funny, for they did not notice it, as they became deliriously sloppy in their behavior. One five top had finished five bottles of wine. A deuce had ten drinks on their tab. Roxi would have loved to 86 them, at least cut them off. She checked with Ned the manager, who because of who they were told Roxi, not to upset any of them, just because they were number one, first of all, celebrating their 50th wedding anniversary, and second the fellow was the mayor of a nearby town.

Roxi aware of it, was reaffirmed that none of these elite people was any better than the average Joe after one or two, too many drinks. "Knowing that the puke of a famous rock singer stinks as badly as anyone else throwing-up in the can." Roxi knew, recalling partying with Joannie and her friends, many years ago. One woman was nearly falling over her own feet. Roxi was able to catch and walk her to the bathroom. She waited for her and accompanied her back to her party and seat.

A rich man was telling jokes which nobody wanted to hear. A famous golf player unstable on his feet was stumbling out the door. The worst part with so many drunks was their lack of bladder control—and more often than Roxi wanted to— she had to replace wet chairs, with a dry seat, six times this shift. The money was good, yet it was very-very unusual to have only heavy drinkers in one station on the same night. Roxi did her very best, yet it was hard on her. She didn't enjoy the scene, and felt sorry for a number of her guests, because the next day, most likely they all woke up feeling sick and bad.

Roxi's last customers left past midnight. As Roxi tipped out, splitting the tips, Ricardo was not only surprised but thanked her, as this night was the largest amount of tips he had ever gotten. She agreed with him.

On her way to the apartment, the one she used to call home, her thoughts were with Ellen, the older frail-looking lady. And she had faith that her applying for housing, done with Ellen's help, will result in getting a nice place at an affordable monthly rent. Roxi was home by 1:30 and in bed, in peace with the world around her, and deep asleep by 2 o'clock.

The third day she slept in, yet was at work by 10 a.m., worked a few tables and a small bus-tour which left by 3:30. The early customers, business folks, had lunch, some small talk, in and out within the hour. After the first seating, as soon as her station was empty, Ned, the manager who filled in for the hostess, had a reservation for a group of 32, for Roxi's station. She worked with Allye, this time, the French waitress on the balcony, an area overlooking the bar below, eight booths holding up to six each. Allye and Roxi worked hand in hand and set each booth for four people. The table settings were for salad, main course, dessert, coffee, soft drinks were included. Booze, each guest had to pay for themselves. Allye added glasses for water, as Roxi folded and placed napkins for each setting.

The group arrived; almost everyone was lining up for the bathrooms before being seated. Roxi had her side-table setup, 32 cold salad plates, Caesar dressing already made, an open can of anchovy and a bowl with croutons. All she had to get was the Romaine lettuce, she picked up a large bowl, of hand broken lettuce leaves in the cold kitchen, already prepared to go by the Filipina cold kitchen chef. Luana with a big smile mentioned: "Fol you, make thilty two olders, and some extra, so you not lun out!" Roxi thanked her. She liked Luana, a hard worker, and a fine lady, working several jobs, to put her two daughters through college.

Arriving with the large bowl of salad, she placed it next to those plates and went to help Allye with serving water, ice tea, lemonade, hot tea and yes there was one cocktail she had to get from the bar. Having taken care of those refreshments, Roxi using a large spoon and fork mixed the dressing with the salad, before dishing it out. Three spoon loads of salad each plate, one anchovy on top and a sprinkle of croutons, and off it went, as Allye four plates at a time served booth after booth. Having some left-over Caesar salad, Roxi put it on a small serving-platter, and walked from table to table and using spoon and fork to serve, offered additional servings. She had only two takers. Both Allye and Roxi cleared the tables, Roxi delivered the empty dishes to the dishwashing area, Diego the main dishwashing guy, with a million-dollar smile, took the full tray out of Roxi's hands, his "Let me do this Miss Roxi, you busy, I do, it's my job." made her smile, he Diego in his late 60s, who had worked at La Casa for more than 15 years, always tried to help and cheer people up. She had never seen him having a bad day. Yet she was sure, he did have such too, but how did he cope so well with all?

The air was heavy with the strong smell of scallops, as she walked past the fish side. Towards the soup and saucier area, a cloud of cognac and wine used for sauces tickled her nose. Such changed as she got closer to the pickup line and the chef's podium. Marti, the Chef de Cuisine, looking at her asking: "Ready to pick up?" got her "Five minutes." answer. His "Ready in five, pick up, Tournedos Rossini fire, thirty-two, I repeat thirty-two fillets, pick up in five, fire!" let everyone in the kitchen know to fire, to cook those steaks now. And five minutes yes just enough time to cook those small steaks all medium to medium-rare. It also let the sauce cook know, to get ready, as well as the cook doing the veggies. On piping hot plate after hot plate, a slice of toasted baguette in Madeira sauce, topped with a small fillet-steak, garnished with foie gras and truffles, a small bunch of green beans wrapped in bacon on one side and two Pommes Croquette on the other side. With eight plates under metal covers on each tray Roxi made four trips to deliver the food up to the balcony. As she left each tray on one of the service tables, Allye served the food and attended to additional drinks.

Done with the main course, while Allye cleared the plates, Roxi was letting the chef know that the dessert can be picked up any time. The Chef de Cuisine was shaking his head, "We try to get those out in ten!" And he walked around the different stations making sure that all ovens were empty. As it was towards the end of lunch service, all ovens were available for the desserts. Roxi didn't hear him, neither did Ned, the manager, yes Marti did cuss because you don't sell thirty-two soufflés to a party. It's not a party dessert. It's something for a four-top, maybe an eight-top, but thirty-two, that's crazy, near impossible to get out in a timely manner. The soufflés went in the ovens, to come out of the ovens perfect — all powder-sugar-coated each on a bed of raspberry coulis. On warm plates, thirty-two soufflés got served and inhaled by each and everyone in the tour group, who all enjoyed the light and airy dessert. Talking with the tour guide, Roxi found out that the luncheon was the tour's good-bye-meal, at the end of a four-week luxury boat and bus trip, one week at the East-coast, one week on a cruise ship, through the Panama Canal, before spending fourteen days of sightseeing on the West-coast by bus. Once finished with the lunch, the bus tour left for a final get-together at their hotel, where a slide-show, coffee and petit fours were waiting. It was about 4 p.m. when Roxi left work, home just about an hour, just enough time to shower, to get into a new set of work-clothing and back to La Casa. This time, to help with a wedding party, and as they were booked for dinner in Hattie's room, and dance in the Wine Room, Roxi expected to stay till the morning hours.

She didn't know that Bernd had arrived early and done all the set up for the party of 28. Roxi arrived late. Her bow tie was somewhat hanging the sloppy way half-tied, half-untied. Her hair had become undone too. "What happened?" Bernd asked.

"I miscalculated the time it takes to walk from my place to the La Casa."

"So?"

"Sorry, but I ran the last mile because I didn't want to be late." Guilt was written all over Roxi's face.

"Get yourself together. Our party arrives in fifteen minutes or less."

Roxi disappeared into the bathroom, while Bernd set up two trays with two dozen sherry and port-wine glasses, into twelve he poured sweet Port wine from Porto in Portugal and the other twelve dry Sherry from Jerez in Spain. Roxi appeared just in time to see the front door open and the first carload of the party guest arriving. Roxy greeted the arrivals with a "Dry Sherry?" as Bernd holding the sweet red asked "Port from Porto?" Slowly more people arrived, the kids wanted Shirley Temples, the bride's mother asked for a screwdriver. Roxi handed her Sherry tray to Bernd and got those orders from the bar. Another older gentleman wanted something, anything nonalcoholic, she got him a glass of pineapple juice. As Bernd kept on offering Sherry or Port wine, Roxi was getting all specialty drinks, and there were quite a few. What Bernd loved about Roxi so much, it was her being of service, not asking twice, but getting whatever was needed to please the customers. Bernd smiled thinking, "A good waiter should not be seen, but be there as and when needed. That's our Roxi to a T."

After having served two rounds of before-dinner drinks, it was time for the party to be seated. While the guests all followed the bride and groom up the steps into Hattie's room, Bernd and Roxi used the back stairs and arrived just about the same time in the party room as the newlyweds. They lit the candles in the four candleholders placed between the five low-flower-arrangements. It was the bride's questioning about the ghost "Have you seen Hattie lately. She is known to be seen on many occasions since the 18th century, when she died in her sleep in front of the fireplace in this room." Roxi made a surprised face, Bernd wasn't sure what to say. The groom helped out, "Ned, the manager told us everything about Hattie, the house-ghost. That's why we asked for an extra chair, that one we keep open, for Hattie's ghost to join us, if she feels thirsty!" Roxi had to force herself not to laugh. Bernd's "What a splendid idea!" was all he said, as by now all seats around the long table but one were taken.

Earlier, starting before 3 o'clock, Bernd had taken care of setting the table, as well as stocking the waiters' station. He had arrived at the La Casa about the time when Roxi and Allye were serving main courses to their tour-group. He had kept the doors to Hattie's room closed and brought all his supplies up using the elevator, that's why Roxi hadn't seen him earlier.

Seeing that all was ready, was a big surprise for Roxi, the white wines were chilled, Champagne was iced, and several red wine bottles were opened, and a decanter was handy should it be needed. Roxi opened five bottles of the local Champagne, realizing these bottles were chilled quite well. "Yes, the cheaper the bubbly, the colder, the better." Off she went, pouring American made Champagne for everyone, except the gentleman who had previously asked for nonalcoholic drinks as well as the kids. For those, she got small bottles of Ginger Ale. By the time she had finished pouring drinks, Bernd with the help of one of the cooks had brought up from the kitchen all twenty-seven shrimp-cocktails on large oval-trays. They placed those on tray-stands, ready to be served. After a speech by the bride's mother, who had since arrival finished three screwdrivers, and was now on her third glass of sparkling wine, they served the shrimp cocktails. It was the bride's mother who insisted, "I see Hattie hasn't made it yet, but please make sure her glasses are always filled, just like mine!" Bernd's "Yes mam!" and Roxi's "Sure shall do!" confirmed that they were on board with whatever the lady wanted. The party of twenty-seven real people, plus Hattie the ghost, was from the get-go a real happy bunch, lots of laughter, plenty of chatting and all in all enjoying themselves a lot. They cleared the appetizer plates, Bernd carried the dishes down and returned with a tray loaded with the main course, hot plates with metal covers stacked three high. Behind him a cook and Diego, the head dishwashing person, with additional full trays. Roxi stopped refilling empty glasses and helped with getting those real hot plates served. Under the metal-covers was Breast of Duck Confit, on a bed of a Zinfandel based red wine sauce, red cabbage, and Pommes Dauphine. As Bernd refilled the breadbaskets, Roxi poured Zinfandel for all who opted for red wine, including the missing ghost, Hattie, who had not yet shown up.

While all were eating, next door in the adjacent room, a band of four older gentlemen were tuning their instruments. That's where the party was supposed to move for dancing into the night. Six round tables, each seating six, were placed around the parquette, the dance floor. Barely done with the main course, some of the guests left and joined the band in the Wine Room. Not long after, all of them had moved to the other side, not wasting any time.

Both, Roxi and Bernd, understood and were flexible when it came to serving ice-cream cake and whoever wanted it, coffee or tea. Everybody had dessert. Only two had coffee. Nobody ordered tea. After the dessert plates were all cleared, and everybody had drinks, both Bernd and Roxi started to clear the party table in Hattie's room. Both stopped at Hattie's chair and looking at the glasses they had filled earlier, all were empty. "Did Hattie follow the invite and had a drink with the wedding party?" Bernd asked. Roxi nodded her head, "Good possible!"

While the folks were having a good time in the Wine Room, dancing to the band playing yesterday's tunes, Bernd with Roxi's help put Hattie's room back to its regular configurations and seating arrangements. It was around midnight when one of the ladies who, not using the upstairs bathrooms, had gone downstairs and used the much larger, more decorative, antique style powder room. As she returned, she let everyone know, "I saw Hattie in a white gown floating through the hall and up the stairs." To the question "What did she look like?" she answered, "She wasn't an old lady, but young and pretty, and seemed to be having had a few drinks too many, as she tried to keep her balance."

Bride and groom left by taxi, at midnight. The rest of the party stayed past 1:30 in the morning. By 2:30 a.m., everyone had left.

Bernd and Roxi had finished resetting the Wine Room for next day's luncheon. The last thing they did was making sure all windows were closed and locked. Bernd talked about waiting for her in the parking lot because he felt like lighting up a joint. Roxi was using the bathroom upstairs. Done, she washed her hands. In leaving, she found the bathroom door resisting her attempts to push it open. "Bernd is this you?" she shouted, not used to her friend playing games with her. There was no answer. Throwing all her weight against the door, it opened. No sign of Bernd either. She was turning off the upstairs' lights, all of them, using the upstairs-main-switch. In the half-dark, Roxi found her way downstairs. She was first bewildered, then shocked as she walked into a cloud of cold air. The staircase and downstairs were well lit, but she couldn't see anything, nothing. She stood there frozen in place, glued to the step, unable to do anything aside feeling the sweat running down her back. Then suddenly a warm cloud-like fog surrounded her, it was dissipating fast. Then all was back to normal except her. Roxi left through the back door, Bernd was getting ready to go home, saying "...goodnight Roxi, I am tired today, time to catch some Zzzz."

She wasn't sure if she should tell him about the scary moments, minutes earlier. Walking home, because she had not brought a car, she was glad she didn't tell Bernd, at her age, people do get strokes and what-have-you. If Bernd thought she was unfit to do the required work, and maybe told Ned, the manager, she could quickly lose her fulltime hours and benefits. As she walked faster, she noticed she was bathed in sweat, all wet, her blouse sticking to her back, her pants sticking to her thighs. It was close to three when Roxi got home, she took a shower, did a dozen basic body exercises, to prove to herself that she was okay. Realizing that Hattie the ghost may be a real occurrence, a phenomenon, she accepted it as such.

Roxi was tired but happy. She didn't even check her email, just went to bed, and in her sleep was dreaming about meeting Hattie and her lucky streak.

The daily income on those past three days, much more than she had ever made on tips in a week.

Chapter 15
Search for a place to live

Upon waking up, her body was aching, and she did need the next day, all day, to recover from those long hours of work. It also was that when she worked upstairs, yes there was the service elevator, she used the stairs. That's why she felt like having been running a slow marathon. Roxi was looking at being off for four days unless she got a call from the Triples Hotel or a good fare through PickMeUp, worth her time. "Am I getting picky, or what?" She asked herself because when broke and hungry, she would take any job to eat and pay rent, and to have some gasoline for Mathilda. She was thinking back at the last time when she had access to lots of money. Shaking her head, she could have done so well if she would have stayed at the Mountain Inn. It was the money, when she had a regular good and steady income, she wanted more, and more, couldn't get enough. Joannie was a customer, and it was Joannie's money which led her astray. She became a party girl. Joannie jokingly offering to marry her, sounded good. Why not a woman? After all, she had been treated not good at all, by her previous two marriages to men. Yes, she had learned her lesson. Come hell or high water she was not going to give up the benefits and good-paying job at the La Casa, for an affair with money, women or men. To take care of herself she had breakfast at a coffee-shop, steak, eggs and pancakes. Thereafter she directed Mathilda to a nearby secluded beach, on a private property. She hadn't been there for some time, yet nothing had changed, the sand was white, much lighter in color and less coarse than most other beaches in the area. Roxi hadn't brought a bathing-suit, only an old beach towel, that one she kept in the car, for such occasions. Soaking in the sun in the nude, cooling off in the water, and more sunning, she succeeded with having a perfect day off. Until the reality started to bother her, the "You need to go and find a place to live!" Telling herself, I shall do so tomorrow, today it is my health and fitness day.

On the following day off, energetic and adventurous, looking for a place to live, Roxi stopped at any place she saw a sign saying 'For Rent' all within 30 minutes of her work. Reason being, half an hour during regular traffic, as the limit for travel time, to work or home, made a lot of sense. Anything more than one hour travel, to and from work was not worth considering, especially when working split shifts, which were typical for wait people. Roxi knew the likelihood to find a place to live, without putting in some effort by searching for it, was very limited. Therefore she was doing her part, the knocking on doors. And she inquired about rentals with the apartment managers wherever the same was on the property and available. As she visited various apartment complexes, she told herself that yes she made good money right now. At the rate she was making money lately, she could pay high rent. However, she knew just too well, those days of unusual good tips and having plenty of work were not guaranteed. By early afternoon she had seen more than one handful of rentals. The more time she spent, looking at places for rent, the more disappointed she got. After seeing eight managers of apartments with 'For Rent' signs, and haven't found one yet in her price range of $1000 to 1500 dollars, that's for a one-bedroom apartment, she was ready to give up. Roxi started to realize her destiny was going to be at street-level, sidewalk, or some dark parking lot.

Looking through the newspaper adds, she did see an apartment, this one was advertised in the newspaper as the most affordable, luxurious, one-bedroom apartment. Roxi went there, it was an older 4 unit complex, in the back of a home. The sign saying "apartment for rent, and inquire within was very promising as well." Then Roxi found out the rent was going to be $2000, moving in she needed $4000, being first and last, as well as a $500 cleaning deposit, in cash or cashier's check. Yes, Roxi had some cash on hand, but no, not this kind of money.

Around the corner another "1 bedroom for rent" sign. One very nice and friendly lady, the apartment manager of this newer apartment complex showed her the advertised, nice one-bedroom apartment, saying: "It's bargain-priced. The same in Oakland is over $3000 a month, in Los Angeles about the same or more, and in San Francisco a lot more." Roxi wondered, "So, how much a month?"

"Only $2450 a month, plus utilities. See if you sign a long term lease you pay only $2250 a month. However, if you break the lease, there is a fine, it equals three months' rent." When the manager handed Roxi an application package, she took it. She thanked the witch. Roxi was ready to leave dreamland and to return to planet earth. As she was on her way back to the place she used to consider home, it felt like nothing more but a temporary shelter. Many thoughts went through her mind while driving towards Spaghetti Hill. She considered sleeping in her VW bus. She had done so before on vacation trips. It was okay, but not comfortable at all. The living outdoors in the local moderate climate sounded not only possible but most likely the only solution to her, the more she thought about it. On second thought: "What about a bathroom, taking a shower to freshen up before work and between shifts?" she asked herself and considered "I can take Marlissa up on her offer, use her place, the tiny little studio, to change for work," but in reality this wasn't such a good idea.

Then again: She did sleep outdoors way back in her hippie days, didn't she? But this now was, at first of all a long time ago, it was much different. Now she had a good job. She needed an indoor place, not outdoor, not too far from her job. Then she contemplated "Not having a place to sleep, and therefore having no job, time to get the revolver. Fred's revolver may be the solution to take herself out of this miserable situation. No, not by shooting herself, but by changing professions, by becoming a bank robber, renting a comfortable mobile home, and traveling the states in search for banks with cash on hand, ready to hand over." Roxi caught herself laughing about such a silly idea. But then again she had all her mother's wigs, up on the shelf in the 2nd bedroom closet.

Chapter 16
Move but where

Feeling good, feeling productive, pleased about her good fortune, the having work, making some money, Roxi got ready to pack up more of the clothing she didn't need. Whereto? Roxi remembered that Richard fellow, the one over there in what used to be called Chinatown, the fellow cooking food for the homeless at The Place. Once she had nine boxes packed and loaded in her car, she took to the road. Getting to Chinatown, slowly down Front Street lined with homeless folks, living in tents, on mattresses or directly on the concrete of the sidewalk, she got to The Place where she had dropped her donations off last time. Roxi drove in 1st gear, slow, having some hope to spot Nicole, her friend, the woman Richard said lived here before leaving town, with some guys in a motorhome. Finding a parking spot next to the door, near the sign saying The Place, Roxi started unloading boxes, and like the other time helping hands were there to bring it all inside. Roxi's question: "Is Richard here?" was answered with "No, he is up in the city today, back tomorrow!" The woman who had said so introduced herself as Carolyn. She invited Roxi to sit down. Guessing that the same hadn't had lunch because of the noise Roxi's stomach made, she went and brought Roxi a bowl of lentil soup and a slice of homemade cornbread. It was delicious. Roxi ate.

Then finally, Roxi introduced herself. Carolyn knew already that she had donated some clothing the other week. "There is more to come if you want it!" Roxi said. Carolyn was happy about the idea because the need seemed to be never-ending. Roxi listened when Carolyn talked about the homeless situation: "Look out the window, the fellow who just got out of that older utility van, over there across the street. He used to be a big shot. He got sued and lost it all. Now he is living in his van and working as a security guard. He is a fine man, sometimes the cards dealt are not as expected." Roxi enjoyed every bit of the tasty lentil soup and used the cornbread to cleanse the soup bowl as she listened to Carolyn. "We have quite a few, who used to live in fine places, at some time they ran out of money, no place to go, but the street...." Carolyn stopped in in the middle of her talk, and introduced an older lady as Dorothy, who was joining the conversation: "I had no place to go. My husband died; he didn't leave anything but debt for me. Conveniently he had forgotten to tell me that we are broke before he croaked."

Turning to Roxi, Dorothy introduced her friend Andy with, "...here on our street at least a dozen people, they came from jail. No place to go, no money for an apartment, nobody willing to take them in, waiting to get some income, willing to do anything to get off the street, but their past is not easy on them. Never mind that they have remorse, have done their time, just like my Andy," and she pointed at a fellow with a long near white beard, all smiling, probably about the same age as Roxi, but hard to guess, who was standing behind Dorothy.

Andy, when being asked about the two older women in the tent next to his, "...they, both Eileen from Idaho and Sylvia from Main, they were teachers, educators all their life. They never paid into Social Security. Both came out here to get away from ice and snow. After a short time, they ran out of money, couldn't pay the rent, having little income, their only choices were, go back home or stay here and camp, live outdoors."

Both Andy and Dorothy went to get a bowl of soup, and several slices of cornbread, returning they joined Carolyn and Roxy at the big round table, with enough space for six or even eight people.

It was Carolyn who offered more of the lentil dish, and Roxi, hungry as she was, followed her to a large soup pot, on the restaurant size stove in the kitchen outbuilding, annexed to the large meeting room. The stock-pot size, multipurpose pot was about half-full with the simple, but nourishing lentil dish. It looked colorful most likely made with brown, yellow, and red lentils.

Carolyn disclosed the secret recipe "...it is in the base and the process of onions, ham hocks, carrots, tomatoes, and garlic, cooked in for hours, the lentils and veggies all added later, the pot filled up with water and letting it cook overnight." Roxi having learned about sauces back at the Mountain Inn, agreed as she refilled her bowl "It's an excellent soup, rich flavorful, the right color, smell, taste..." and yes Roxi found a small piece of meat hidden in the thick soup dish as well. Carolyn had a good point when she talked about young men and women, who once they get stranded on the streets have a hard time to get back on their feet. "They can't get an education either. As getting an education can run them easily in the many-many thousands. And if they had the money, they wouldn't be broke, and homeless."

Another couple, in their late twenties, early thirties Tom and Nelly, were welcomed by all. And after getting their lentil soup too, they become part of the discussion at the round table. All were talking about living on the street.

Nelly's, "...those of us, who need medication have difficult times to pay for it, such too can be astronomical..." got Andy going "...there is limited medical care. As you all may know, none of my friends here can afford to see any of those $1000 concierge doctors and concierge medicine-men..." They all laughed, obviously the idea to pay a $1000 copay to see a doctor, in these circles, was nothing but a bigtime joke.

Than Carolyn looking out the window, she talked about a young woman walking past the entrance of The Place and Roxi's VW bus, "...that's Cheryl, she has lost most of her teeth. She has been trying now for over six months to get some dentures."

Nelly added to the conversation, "...don't we have decent habitats for wildlife, we have parks and recreation areas for every kind of animal, but none for us and our friends, who are forced to live here on the street."

Tom agreed with her, "It would be easy to help us, to provide spaces like campgrounds with showers and toilets for all those who have no place to stay, as an interim solution, and allow us to gather the needed strength to start over, but no, society is forcing us into areas like here, or into fenced-in areas, being kicked around too many times, and what next?"

Andy obviously thinking it would be a great idea, says, "...we are all humans, why can't we camp out near a river, near lakes, eat on a picnic table, catch fish, eat a deer, a rabbit, or a boar, have showers, bathrooms, and enjoy what was freely given to us, the land, the country of the free. We are treated worse than murderers and criminals. They at least have a dry place to sleep, get free breakfast, lunch, and dinner, as well as medical attention, and education as well. But here on the street, we are watched day and night like we are the bad guys, which we aren't."

Roxi asked: "Isn't there plenty of space in one of those wide-open areas we have in this country, doesn't have to be ranch land, or farmland, or the main beach of any town, nor any one of those plentiful gated communities with golf courses, but isn't there some federal and state land which could be used to allow people to camp out for free, just to have a spot to live, while being in a bad spot? See, in the eighties, people slept along the road, the highway, lived in the redwoods, had teepees on government and sometimes private land, it was okay, we then hippies were never forced to live in ghettos like here, crammed together on asphalt and concrete."

Carolyn answered her with "...there is plenty of space, much is fenced in, with signs saying no trespassing..." and "...the open areas like along the ocean, on the beach, nobody wants the tourists to take pictures of homeless people, after all, we are living in America, the most wealthy country, the home of the rich and mighty US dollars."

"What is the real reason that homeless people are herded together, in some areas behind fences, away from the local population?" Roxi wondered while finishing her second bowl of lentil soup.

"Safety in numbers, many of our friends who have no place to call home, have been chased away, have been threatened by law and whatever other means. Asked to get lost too often, and if they didn't leave, where they had hoped to spend a day, a night a few days, heavy equipment, herds of animals, or other threats to their lives scared them, to move on. They are afraid, that's what safety in numbers is about," was Carolyn's answer, and Nelly, Andy, Dorothy, as well as Tom, agreed.

Andy, while shaking his head, "...it hurts when we have to watch what people do to their fellow men. Have you seen the times they clean the street here, within a day's notice we all have to leave, no place to go to. Have no means to carry the little we have, even on a bicycle, or in a shopping cart. We can only take so much, so little with us. Then the street cleaning crew and the trash-men take away what's left, garbage to them, treasures to so many of us homeless folks."

Looking in Roxi's eyes Andy in a sad voice, while picking some run-a-way lentils from his long white beard,

"...do you know how it feels when you get back to the spot you called home, and there is nothing there, the plastic crate you left, the one which was your bookshelf and bedside table, gone. The bucket you used as a toilette, gone. The three one gallon water bottles, your water supply, gone. The blanket and pillow you couldn't carry, gone..."

And digging into the history books Dorothy reminded all, "...either America hasn't learned from the Trail of Tears, or we all have started to get stoic, unemotional about the suffering of our fellow men, who because we are different, nobody wants us around."

Carolyn agreed that it was a sad state of affairs, situations, and circumstances. "It's not just about a street filled with people in need of assistance. We have over ½ million homeless people, that's the official number, unofficial it's a lot more. It's nothing to laugh about, and getting worse..." Andy nodded his head. Dorothy opening one of the water bottles Tom had gotten for the table, "The biggest problem is that many of us when we are down and out, we forget who we are, being treated worse than animals, we soon start to believe that we are as bad as we feel..." and she takes a sip of the bottled water.

Andy was with her, "...no wonder that so many people on the streets after a short while, start looking for drugs or anything to take the pain away, the pain of being a nothing, the pain of being a loser, the pains of being no good."

Carolyn was blaming greed, "Look at some real rich places, just like here. For example, San Francisco and Silicon Valley, or Los Angeles, all places with lots of money, and visitors, just see how many humans are living on the streets, in their cars or on the sidewalks."

"And yes, there are those who blame the fast growth of the homeless population on mental illness; it wasn't too long that the federal government decided to close mental illness institutions? Remember? They called it deinstitutionalizing!" Nelly commented with a sad face.

"Then others blame it all on drugs and alcohol. The truth for the drug addict or alcoholic is that they have programs which can lead them back to become a useful member of society."

Carolyn's, "Let's blame everyone, but not those who have caused it, greedy landlords, the profit-hungry investors. It's neither drugs nor alcohol, or mental illness when employees in many places, can find plenty of work, but no place to raise their families, not even a place to find rest for the night, unless they have a car where to go to sleep between shifts worked..."

...and she asked, "How many low-income earners, who make $2500 a month, can afford a $2000 plus, one-bedroom apartment?"

"Have you noticed how hostile home and landowners do everything they can to remove or make it hard on the homeless near their places?" Tom wondered.

"The saying of, not in my backyard, has also become a, not in my front yard, and for some as well, not in my view-shed!" Nelly acknowledged Tom's thoughts.

And none of this talk was doing much for Roxi, and she confessed "After 25 years at the same place, I got a 60-day notice to vacate. I have to move out of my apartment by the end of next month. If I could, I would move sooner.

I have put in applications and more applications. I am a waitress. My tax-return shows how little I make." After taking a deep breath, she carried on, "Right now I have a full-time job, which I haven't had for the past three years, right now my income is good, I even have medical benefits, life is good, the best it has ever been!"

"So what's the problem?" Nelly asked, "What problem?" Tom wanted to know. Here Roxi disclosed, "I have not found an apartment yet. My credit history, personal history, criminal history, and tax returns have caused property managers to laugh at me, and my daring silliness to dream about getting them to rent to someone like me."

"I see..." Carolyn acknowledged "...these are the ingredients to the mixture which has brought many of our friends in the door right here, for a meal, for a smile, a conversation, an uplifting moment of hope."

Deep in thought, Roxi left The Place, Carolyn, and her new friends. The session of hive-minded people, collective thoughts shared, made her feel better, as she visualized sleeping in her VW bus. However, she wondered how hard it might be to get a parking spot close to the front door of The Place. From what she saw, there was nothing available. All spots were already taken.

Chapter 17
Getting worse

As Roxi got home, her phone was playing the money-money song. It was Hans from the Triples Hotel, once again, he needed help, "Can you come in tonight, please? Two of my servers have called in sick." She was thinking cash, making some tips, atop of the meager minimum wage per hour and knowing that she liked to work with Hans and Emile. She said, "Yes! When do you want me to be there?"

Hans asked, "It's 4 o'clock now, can you be here at the hotel by 6?"

And with a "See you at 6 o'clock!" Roxi hung up. Roxi eager to make some money, knowing that from experience the Triples Hotel jobs meant beaucoup bucks in the pocket, she showed up for work, on time and ready for a busy night. Hans had given her the Library Room, and two a la carte parties, one of eight at 7 o'clock and a second party of twelve at 9 o'clock. It was a race weekend. With visitors from all over the world, every hotel room within 50 miles was booked. Restaurants were busy, and for the evenings after the races, it was difficult to get a reservation for dinner, the option was to stand in line and eat at the walk-in dining places. Roxi made sure that she had her service station set up, extra glasses, ice, water pitchers, saucers and cups for coffee, as well as creamers and sugar.

She liked the idea of parties without a preset meal. That Sepp fellow, the German waiter who had trained her, he had told her over and over "Waiting on tables equals working the table." Yes, Roxi liked the á la carte business. She was looking forward to the challenge of selling whatever the Chef Emille recommended. From experience, Roxi knew that any single party of 8 or 12 was easier to handle than five four-tops. She had made a list of those items Chef Emille highly recommended and she was going to push those menu-items because she knew that they were the best the kitchen had to offer. Roxi was all set to do her job to build up the check for those hungry race-fans as soon as they arrived. She was going to make it a good night for her customers, the house, and herself. Roxi knew that she was going to start selling as soon as her group of guests got seated. She was going to take their drink order and not give in on an "I don't drink." answer but push virgin cocktails, non-alcoholic-wines, and alcohol-free beer or juices. Roxi planned on her guests to have appetizers. So was going to tell them about individual orders of appetizer samplers especially made for them by Chef Emille. Aware of the chef's individual platters of finger-licking most-sumptuous hors d' oeuvres one of many of Emille's specialties. Those included the crab cake made from Dungeness crab straight from San Francisco Bay and the King Crab is flown in from Alaska, served with beurre-blanc sauce. Added to it the prawns from Bahia Magdalena California Sur sautéed in Pernod, and next to it tiny pieces of the local Abalone, gently sautéed in unsalted butter. A most delicious arrangement of palate teasing appetizers, known as Emille's Pacific Sampler Starter. Knowing that it takes about fifteen minutes for the sampler-plate to be made, it allowed Roxi plenty of time to get the rest of the order while waiting for those appetizers to arrive. Roxi was ready to provide recommendations for the salad and main course orders too. The reason for her trying to get the full order before serving any food was based on the-hungry-eyes-bigger-than-the-appetite principle. A hungry customer tends to overestimate his appetite and orders a lot more than after he has eaten some appetizers.

Before and during the order-taking of the salads and the main courses, Roxi was going to explain all items in detail. Tonight she was going to tell her customers what they will find in a mixed green salad. She would give a description of the crunchiness of the hearts of Romaine with some French dressing. She was going to disclose to them the ingredients of the Caesar salad and would explain how the spinach salad is made. Knowledgeable about food and food preparation Roxi would let the guests know what Enoki mushrooms are, and where the goat cheese came from. She would not leave any of the specialty salads out, like the chef's special Chinese-style duck salad. Roxi was known to give her guests a money-back guarantee. Her: "If you don't like snails in your salad, I'll eat them." She was used to getting some laughter and a few people asking about snails, and yes there was a special Emille Escargot salad on the menu too. Roxi was used to dealing with the entrée orders in the same way as the salads. She would describe them in an appealing way. Once Roxi knew the guests' food, it was effortless for her to find the matching wines.

Yes, Roxi was ready, all planned out, her expectations were high. Hans came and let her know, "...the eight-top is going to be a table of fourteen and that they may be half an hour late." Roxi got busy moving tables and setting it up for fourteen guests. Done, it was getting closer to 7:30 p.m. The party of fourteen didn't show at 8 o'clock. By 8:30, still a 'no show.'

Roxi still had high hopes to make up with the twelve top at 9 o'clock, it didn't materialize, at 9:30 still no show, and by 10 o'clock they had not arrived. Roxi started to break her station down, no guest - no sales - no money. Hans was telling her that he was sorry, by then it was about 11. Roxi was getting ready to mosey up the hill, to go home. Hans told her what he had found out about those two parties, "They had made reservations at several restaurants, and when leaving the race track, they drew straws to decide what dinner place to dine at. Unfortunately, we were not the winners."

"It's okay Hans!" she said.

"I promise to make it up to you. I know you need the money, you can't afford to stand around all night." That's when she let Hans know that she had quit the Sassy Station & Bar job and that the manager at La Casa has offered her full-time work and benefits. Hans who usually was very conservative, instantly gave Roxi a big hug, and his words "Congratulations, I am so happy for you, that's the best news I have heard for a while," meant a lot for Roxi. However getting home with empty pockets, she started asking herself "What will happen when I turn 70, in five years, when they take me off the schedule at La Casa, because I am too old. Just like they do every place, the old servers being replaced with fresh, young wait-people?" What did she have to show for 65 years of being on this planet? What good had she done, how useful was her being on this earth? Questions she couldn't answer, and with this kind of worries, Roxi felt she wasn't having one of her best days.

*****

The second week of three split shifts, back to back, she had on day one a couple she had waited on at several places over the years. They the Millers were happy to see Roxi, and right away insisted on having her as their waitress. It was a regular Tuesday. For luncheon, very few reservations, a regular day, so to say. The hostess had no problem to seat the Miller couple at a window table in Roxi's section. She had a section of seven tables, at the time however only one was taken, with the Miller's she now had two deuces. Roxi remembered the first time she waited on the Miller couple, which was during a long weekend. Back then, they stayed at a Bed and Breakfast Inn. The Millers visited the peninsula at least once every couple of months, driving all the way from Oakhurst in the High Sierras, near Yosemite. This time the Millers were talking about how beautiful a place they rented for the week. They did not stop talking about the beautiful old furniture and the unbelievable view. The Millers got to watch sea otters in the kelp, and they were so happy about everything happening in their lives. Naturally, they had to ask Roxi how things are going, expecting to hear only praise. It was difficult for Roxi to lie, she couldn't tell them that life had thrown her a curveball, something as unexpected as being put on the street. "I am trying to figure out if I am at or in a midlife crisis, but once I know I let you know," she said with a smile, and it worked. With the menu, the Miller couple was hesitant, studying the fine-print word by word. It was their first visit to the La Casa, but lucky enough there was Roxi, and they both relied upon her guidance. Both asked many questions about preparation and ingredients as to at least half of the menu items. Roxi served the food at the other table and made sure they had everything they needed, before spending more time with Mr. and Mrs. Miller. Now she found out that not only was it Mrs. Miller's 71st birthday, but it was also their 50th wedding anniversary. "That's why Ben took me to the best, and highest-rated, most expensive place in town. So glad he did, because we got to see you, my dear Roxi."

It was some time back that she had served the Millers dinner, and it was down at the wharf, where Roxi used to work at the Clam-House. Mrs. Miller recalled that they both were somewhat reserved to the idea to try soft shell crabs as an appetizer but believed Roxi when she told them it's good. Roxi served their plates but surely noticed the indecision, the questioning look on their faces staring at the food. Neither one of the Millers knew what to do next. Roxi came to their rescue pointing at their plates said, "These soft shell crabs from the East Coast look so much different to what we usually get around here in California, don't they?" Both nodded their heads. He was ready to say something but did not. Mrs. Miller admitted, "I have never seen anything exactly like these." Roxi helped them "The first time I had soft shell crab, I was told to eat the same in one bite." She shared her experience when having the same appetizer. "I did. It was quite a mouthful." Roxi had coached them along with "These days I cut each into four equal pieces." Then Roxi had taught them how to use the sauce, "Then I savor each bite after dunking it into the beurre blanc sauce." To overcome the scary thought of eating guts and shell, "And I eat it all, as is, with the crunchy shell and everything." Mrs. Miller remembered that her husband Ben, and she both did as told. "We loved those critters," she said, "It was on my 65th birthday. Yes, and they were good. Therefore Ben's question "Where do they hide the East Coast Softshell Crabs on this fancy menu?" Roxi had to admit there aren't any on the menu. However we have crab cakes, and they are the best I have ever tried, the chef uses Alaskan king crab and local crabmeat, no filler added. We serve three crab cakes of the size of old fashioned silver coins, on a beurre blanc sauce. Mrs. Miller agreed "Let's try their crab cakes for both of us." They also ordered the Mahi Mahi. It was a large order. Therefore Roxi decided to split it for them, so they would have enough space for a Crème Brulee afterward. Roxi checked with the chef, who was in a good mood. He didn't mind splitting the Mahi Mahi onto two plates, for Roxi's customers. Walking by the table towards a new table of five, Roxi overheard Mrs. Miller telling the couple at the next table "This waitress, she is so nice and helpful. She is the best in town." Roxi's ego got inflated, hearing the praise. It made her feel good.

The new five top was a big deal, the tables next to them got reserved signs, to make sure nobody sat right next to them. Both Ned and the hostess were trying to satisfy the requests of the grey-suit-blue-tie-black-shiny-shoes-guy, the one who insisted on the best table in Roxi's station, as well as making sure that whoever would wait on them, was solely there for them, not running off or taking care of any other guests.

The early deuce in Roxi's station asked for their check, she presented it and ran the credit card.

By now those five at the top VIP table were sipping on cocktails delivered by Robert the bartender himself. The Millers enjoyed their crab cakes and with it some sparkling wine.

Ned, the manager, asked Roxi to hand the Miller table over to Allye, who had the station next to her. Not too happy, but following orders, she did just such. As the fellow who seemed to be in charge at the 5-top waved her over, she greeted him with a: "Yes Sir, Good Afternoon! How can I be of service?" His "What's your name?" She answered, still smiling: "Roxi." The "Okay," from this fellow, didn't have much meaning. Roxi followed it up with: "Please let me know when you are ready for the menu." He talked to the two gentlemen near the window. Now she saw the face of the one on the right. Even with sunglasses, she recognized him as a well-known movie star. Roxi heard the "Don this doll wants to know if you are ready to eat, and what about you, Dave?" She heard the "No, ask the bartender to bring us another round of drinks first," and "...yes get us a drink on the double." Roxi's "I gladly get your drinks. Will it be the same as the first round?" Seeing nodding faces, she went to the bar, got the drinks, served them, only to find out that they had changed their mind, they didn't want a refill, but Champagne instead. Roxi brought the extensive Wine List. They decided on a bottle of the least pricey American Champagne. Roxi found a chilled bottle and served it in an ice-bucket. She showed the bottle's label to the grey-suit-blue-tie-black-shiny-shoes-guy, who had ordered it. He accepted it. Roxi undid the foil, opened the wire cage, and slowly carefully removed the plastic cork. Roxi placed a champagne glass in front of each customer, poured a small sip, enough for a taste for the fellow who had ordered it, and as she was told, "Fill up all the glasses, Doll" she did just such. It was a somewhat happy-go-lucky group of people, two young starlets, the movie-star with dark glasses and a good looking young man, and yes the rude fellow acting like being the host, or maybe the movie star's manager. Roxi was aware that some of the upscale oriented, ego-driven guest think, they can get away with anything, for some of them, after all, waitresses are very low on the totem pole.

The simple people usually tried very hard to be well mannered and were afraid to say or do the wrong thing in upscale dining. And so did the majority of noble-born folks who, in order to keep face attempted to behave according to their upbringing. It was quite common of the nouveau-riche crowd, to behave pushy and arrogant, or just making a point of being different, being special. Some women got their kicks by shocking onlookers while amusing their table partners. True here, Roxi's eyes were several times confronted by the long shaven legs of the two very pretty models being part of the 5-top. Not only the newly rich but also the not so rich can be found to be part of promotional actions in need to be seen, if that was the main idea. Near topless, no underwear as little as possible outerwear, and see-through-blouses or dresses were made for this purpose. If a woman dressed in some expensive outfit that revealed everything beneath, Roxi actually had to admit, it was classy—as long as she had the body for it, and those two young women surely had the frame and anatomy for it.

Roxi's thought was "...hats off to all the ladies rebelling against any buttoned-up open-mouthed close-minded society which adores the nude paintings and statues of old masters but for moral reasons requests that the beauty of a woman's body has to be concealed." No, Roxi wasn't offended by the two young women, neither by the rude host.

Taking a moment to check on her friends the Millers, they were happy about the split order of Mahi, and they also didn't mind Allye, as a fill-in, Ben had noticed the movie star and his entourage, and from the way they acted, and talked. He knew that Roxi was going to have her hands full when he said "Roxi we love you, and appreciate all you do, and your hard work. Those scheisters over there don't deserve you." Roxi smiled about Mr. Miller's words, they warmed her heart, as she was keeping an eye on her special VIPs. She served another bottle of American Champagne and one more. Nearly two hours had gone by when she finally walked over to them with the menus in hand. Asking "Aren't you getting hungry? Would you care to have a look at our menu? We also have a number of specials, may I tell you about those most delectable dishes prepared by our Chef de Cuisine and his crew?" Roxi was all in her element, ready to sell them up and take care of the five-top; after all, it was her only table. It was a genuine disappointment when she found out that he, the grey-suit-blue-tie-black-shiny-shoes-guy had called their order in the previous night, and demanded to get their food now. Roxi checked with the chef, with Ned, and with the hostess. No, nobody had called in any order, last night.

Back to the gentleman, very careful not to create a scene, she did ask him with whom he talked when he placed the order. The gentlemen, not so gentle, pulled out his iPhone and showed her the message he had sent to the restaurant, she copied the phone number and the items as pre-ordered for their 6-course meal. None of the details matched the menu of the La Casa. However, all were international cuisine menu items, such as Oysters on the half shell, Beef Wellington. The one item ordered was a giveaway, Pate Maison Casa Nova, it clicked. Yet not to say something drastic, she said: "I apologize, that something like this happened, and somehow in the ether of the internet, if not HI (human intelligence), then AI artificial intelligence must have failed us" She was trying to be as pleasing as possible as the two young women's eyes were glued to her lips. The three men seemingly just couldn't care less. The grey-suit-blue-tie-black-shiny-shoes-guy, he was not one bit polite as he was telling her in a loud voice "Listen to me, Doll, This must be the worst place in town. The table wasn't ready, still isn't set for our meal. We had asked for privacy, and didn't get it?" Now Roxi had enough. "Sorry to hear this. Sir, can I see the message once more, the one you sent last night for your reservation?" He showed her with a "Here see!" and added, "Listen Doll, we also asked for Champagne, and all we got is some cheap American sparkling wine!"

"Excuse moi, Sir, it looks like you, yourself, or whoever used this your iPhone, made a reservation at the Casa Nova restaurant on the other side of town. When you leave and please have look at the sign outside the front door, you will see this here is the La Casa."

One of the two young women broke out in hysterical laughter, as the host's stern face got longer and he was looking for words to tell Roxi off. She was faster, with a "Since we now established that you are at the La Casa. Please let me know if you want to order here and stay here..." and "...in any case, you may want to call the place where you made your reservation, the Casa Nova, and tell them that you went to the wrong restaurant, because they may not keep your table much longer, since you didn't show up for your reservation!" Yes, Roxi, did say each word loud enough that everyone nearby could hear her, surely everyone at the grey-suit-blue-tie-black-shiny-shoes-guy's table heard it. It was suddenly quiet, not only at the VIP table but at the surrounding tables as well. Roxi, knew immediately that she had overstepped her authority to tell that jerk that he was wrong. She left the table and looked for Ned. By the time he got to the table they had gotten up, and with a "Something went wrong, we should be at the Casa Nova, but ended up here." "It's all the chauffeur's fault." Giving Ned his business card, then the grey-suit-blue-tie-black-shiny-shoes-guy said, "Send me the bill!" and they left, only to come back in to wait for their driver who had parked the limo over at the Casa Nova. Coming to find out that they had arrived in two taxies earlier, but had instructed their chauffeur to pick them up at the Casa Nova. As those five sat at the big round table between entrance door and fireplace, she heard the movie star, blaming the grey-suit-blue-tie-black-shiny-shoes-guy for screwing it all up. Taking the opportunity, Roxi ran the 5-tops check and presented it to the big-mouth-fellow with a "...as you are waiting to be picked up, you may have enough time, to settle the bill for what you ordered. I gladly run your credit card, unless you prefer to pay cash." As the same was going to say something, the young fellow, grabbed the ticket, looked at it, took a wad of money from his pocket, and handed Roxi 2 one hundred dollar bills, after a second look, seeing the total was $175, he said "Please keep the change, and thank you for getting us all those drinks, we may not even get to eat, till dinner tonight."

Roxi went back to see the Miller couple. Mr. Miller complimented Roxi for being so diplomatic with those VIPs, and promised to be back next time. After her lunch shift, Roxi went home, she made on tips, all in all 35 bucks.

Back by 5:30 p.m. she worked again the same station of 7 tables, in the Gallatins dining room. This night Roxi had five tables of foreigners, four were Germans, who because they are used to inclusive pricing, thought the tip was included. Looking at the credit card slips, at the end of her shift, she realized no tip, except one table, a $15 tip.

Home by just about midnight. Roxi told herself, "You win some. You lose some!"

The next day, Wednesday was not much better. Lunch she made $30 in tips.

Dinner, she was to work a party. However the same was canceled and she went home.

And finally, on Thursday. At lunch she made $15.

Dinner, they had too many people scheduled. Roxi went home again.

Had she lost her touch, her abilities to wait on people and make a living?

It just couldn't get worse, or could it? Less than $100 in three days, the total income for a week.

Chapter 18
Rosemary

After the miserable week, last week, the next week was back to normal. Not overwhelming, but okay.

Roxi had finished another three days of double shifts, lunch, and dinner. She was by now used to working those long hours. She was happy about her job at the La Casa, yet felt bad about her inability to find an apartment. No, she had not given up but surely felt like there was little or no choice, none whatsoever. Roxi did admit that she had been a screw-up, most of her life. If she had married a rich man, she might now be living in a castle, worrying about what jobs to give her maid, her gardener, her chauffeur.

Then she caught herself laughing aloud "So why would I want to spend my life in a golden cage?" and "I want to be free, so I am!" and "Here I am!" Deep in thought, she went and picked up her mail from the mailbox. An envelope with stamps from Denmark arrived, eagerly she opened it. The content a prepaid roundtrip via Lufthansa, and a reminder that the invitation was real. Roxi wondered, "If I have no place to live, sell my VW bus, get on a plane to Denmark, can I get a job there? Can I make a living there? Those two Claus and Freja are nice people. How long will they put up with Roxi? What if I end up without a job, without a place to live in Denmark?" Doomsday thoughts galore, a human intelligence experience, filled with cognitive distortions nothing but catastrophic thinking, expecting the worst to happen, without being able to consider other possibilities, filling Roxi's space between her ears.

She was brought back to reality by the ring-ring of a phone call. Roxi wasn't interested in talking with anyone, at least not with somebody not listed in her address and phone book. Still, she looked at the iPhone's display. It showed 'City Housing Authority.' Roxi answered the call in a hurry. Not expecting much, aside from being turned down once more, once again. A friendly voice announced herself as Rosemary, from City Housing.

She asked Roxi: "Are you ready to come and see your new apartment?"

"What? Really? You have an apartment for me?" Roxi's voice-tone didn't hide her being in awe, astonished, totally surprised before she started crying and had difficulties in forming understandable words.

The voice on the phone talked about rental agreement, use of laundromat, eviction clauses and much more, including the monthly rent and the last month deposit. Roxi heard it but was unable to remember one word, as it all went in one ear, out the other. The lady on the phone a Rosemary, expected to meet Roxi this same morning, in about an hour at a city-owned apartment building at Portuguese Hill. Roxi was at the address given to her within less than 20 minutes. A lovely older apartment building, it looked promising. Still, Roxi wondered: "What's the catch?" It wasn't long that a car with city stickers on the doors arrived. The lady getting out was about Roxi's age, was smiling, coming right over to her, stating: "You must be Roxi, I am Rosemary!"

After meeting Rosemary in the parking lot, not wasting any time, the city housing employee took Roxi to a large one-bedroom apartment.

She asked: "What is your relationship with Ellen?"

Before Roxi could answer, Rosemary, let her know that Ellen had called her every day, to get Roxi a place, not only did she call, in church sitting next to her Ellen, was holding her hand and praying to God for a place to live, for her friend Roxi. Now Roxi was speechless. She barely knew the woman. All she could say: "Thank you, thank you. I love my new apartment. Yes, Ellen is a good woman."

Rosemary handed her some paperwork. And she needed it back, all signed before Roxi could move in. On the other paper, there was the address where she was expected to send the monthly check to. Roxi heard Rosemary saying: "Call me if you need anything!" But she couldn't see anything, Roxi's blue eyes were overflowing with tears. Rosemary gave her a big hug, then pressed her business card, the apartment keys, and the mailbox and laundromat keys into her hands, and with a "Talk to you later..." off she went.

Roxi was trying to take it all in, without getting hysterical, and without screaming and alarming the neighbors that a real crazy one, a true kooky had arrived.

She stood at the kitchen counter, looking at papers Rosemary had left with her, there was the rental agreement with the city. She realized that her rent was only $800 a month, affordable and cheap compared to what similar apartments rented for in these days of a tight housing market. Aside from everything else, now she could start saving money and stop worrying about where to sleep. Overwhelmed like a little kid seeing her gifts, delivered by Santa Claus, the first time, she walked around her new place, her home. She admired her new kitchen with gas stove, a microwave, a dishwasher, a new large refrigerator and icemaker, and not to forget the small pantry, hidden in a walk-in-closet, accessible from the kitchen. The living room was small, with a glass sliding door leading out onto a balcony with a distant view of the Pacific. The bathroom was clean, older, but had aside the claw-foot-tub, an enclosed shower as well. The bedroom was just big enough for her bed, the California King she was used to sleeping on.

Behind a mirror-covered door, a good size walk-in-closet. Plenty of space for clothes as well as some boxes.

Yes, this was a nice size one-bedroom apartment, Roxi was excited. For a moment, she thought about moving in, right then, on the very same day. Happy, she went to her old place of residence, raided her cookie jar, the one where she had all the tips from this month. Counted 1600 dollars, and put the rest back. Roxi drove over to the City Housing Authority and paid both the first month's rent and the last month's deposit in cash. She also brought all the papers in need of signing along. Within an hour it was official, another hug from Rosemary sent Roxi home, to plan the moving out from Mr.Ventura's place, and moving in at her own new nest.

*****

Next, she went to see Ellen, no she wasn't in. Roxi was told, by a young man, to come back in two weeks, as by then Ellen was expected to be back at work.

Roxi went home. Here she was making plans as to what to take, what to donate for a good cause and what to move. There was so much she wasn't going to take with her to her new place. Whatever she thought her friends at The Place might be able to use, she was going to take to Carolyn. Roxi boxed up the raincoats, the winter clothing once belonging to her mother, shoes and more shoes, for a trip to see her friends at The Place. On her iPad finally, an email she thoroughly enjoyed, it was from Claus and Freja, telling her that they had arrived safely at home. Freja was thanking Roxi for spending time with them and the tour into 'God's country' and the snacks, and the history lessons. Then Freja asked, if she doesn't mind, and provided the publisher accepts it, she would like to print a few paperbacks of the manuscript in both English and Danish. Claus insists on using one of the Santa Lucia mountain ridge photos for a cover. All at no cost to Roxi. No guarantees, but Claus and Freja thought such would be a freaking out good idea. And Claus asked if the airline ticket had arrived.

Roxi all pumped up, filled with enthusiasm and excitement, answered the email with a "Please, yes please do so, love you both, yes ticket arrived today, can't come now, am moving, but if offer is good for later in year, after the tourist season, I come and visit. Roxi."

And with plenty of energy, she packed up unneeded clothing, emptying much of her mother's closet. Two calls for fares she ignored, another trip to The Place, the giving to the needy and showing that she cared, even if nobody else cared was more important to her. With a load ready to be donated, she was ready and on the road to The Place.

Chapter 19
the gun

Back from dropping of clothing at The Place, Roxi sat down ready to plan her move, but not without talking to Chris. She told her iPhone "Siri call Chris!" and once Chris answered, she asked him about his schedule, and if he still was going to help her with the move.

"Yes, Miss Roxi, it shall be a pleasure," he said.

To make sure that he would know what to move to the new apartment and what to haul away to the dump, Chris offered to stop by the same evening.

Chris arrived looked around and listening to Roxi saying: "This goes, that doesn't go, these go, no go!" Chris was making his list of what to move. Making his notes, Chris stood there at the kitchen counter, while Roxi searched under the mattress for the gun, the old revolver, the one once hidden in Fred's trunk.

Roxi's "This one too has to go; I don't need it!" got his attention.

She handed it to him, holding it with both hands at the barrel. "...it's a heavy one.." she warned him, "...oh no, what is it made off?" he asked, as it slipped out of his hand and hit the concrete kitchen floor. With a "Sorry, but..." he picked it up. One of the grips now showed underneath the black paint a golden color. Chris, in disbelieve, looking at what he saw, didn't hear Roxi's "Can I sell this gun someplace? It's surely antique, I think! Any idea what it's worth? Can I get 50 or 100 bucks for it?"

Chris, had taken the revolver over to the sink, busy with a pot scrubber, he cleaned the black paint of both grips, said "Roxi, this looks to me like gold." Then using a knife, he cut into it. "Yes it's gold, there is something special about this revolver, and it doesn't have a pin at the hammer, and wouldn't work as a gun in the first place!"

"You say, it doesn't work!" and "So it's worthless?" Roxi's "What do suggest?" had Chris taking a closer look at the parts of the revolver. He was able to unscrew the barrel, then removed the cylinder too. He pushed the cartridge casings out, and looked at them in total disbelief.

Chris told her, "I would suggest you take these parts here to one of the people who buy gold and get an estimate as to the value."

"Gold, it's not just painted? You sure?"

"As sure as my name is Christopher, aka Chris."

"Can you do this for me, let's say for a finder's fee?" She asked him in a begging voice, and adding "When they see a woman they always try to cheat, but when a man shows up those jewelry and gold buy and sell people have much more respect."

"Yes, Roxi, if you trust me with so much gold." Chris mentioned, "Getting a finder's fee, I could use the money, we have a hospital bill we cannot pay, I have been thinking about bankruptcy. Any cash will help, to keep the collection agencies at bay," and he handed two revolver parts, the barrel and the cylinder to Roxi.

"Feel how heavy it is, like lead, but see the color, that's gold."

"Chris, I never paid for the gun. My ex-husband Fred, who is dead, he left it here."

And looking at Chris, she said "Let's make it 50-50! Whatever they pay us for the gold, half is yours!" and looking in Christopher's eyes, she asked, "Deal?"

"Really, you are not kidding?" a near speechless Chris asked. Laughing, she pressed the golden gun parts back into his hands, saying, "Just let me know about the outcome."

No, Roxi had no interest in the gun, glad she didn't try to shoot anyone, including this Steve guy with it because now she knew that it wouldn't have worked.

"Now when do you want me to move your belongings?" Chris asked.

"How about next Saturday? I work Tuesday, Wednesday and Thursday double shifts. On Friday I can pack boxes all day, if you move me on Saturday, I have Sunday to clean the old place, and Monday to put things away at the new apartment."

"For you, I do a Saturday move anytime," he said, "about the gold…" pointing at the revolver in the plastic shopping bag "…I let you know as soon as I know more."

After Chris left, Roxi started to make a list of whom to see and call to make her move a success, first getting her electricity put in her name at the new place, than to get the internet router and modem moved and last the postman, even she got most mail at her Post Office mailbox, still some people had her address for so many years and always sent her some mail, like greetings, to where she lived. The same was true for her absentee voting papers. Roxi slept well this night, in her dreams she asked herself, "...is it true, is this all happening, or am I going crazy, and it's all nothing but a fantasy?"

After getting up, no makeup, wearing old jeans and a sweater, she treated herself to breakfast at a fast-food-place, just across the street from her new apartment. After finishing her orange juice, the medium rare steak, and three eggs sunny side up, toast and marmalade, she took a walk over to her still empty nest. She enjoyed the good feeling of her new apartment, walked around, met two of her neighbors, just making sure that it all was real, and she wasn't dreaming. Then she left.

Arriving at her old apartment, ready to pack up items she no longer needed. The night owl sounds on her phone indicated a friend was calling. Roxi answered. It was Chris, "Sit down Roxi," he said.

"Okay, what happened," she asked.

"Mr. Felix, who buys gold, is giving you 50 grand for the gold."

"50 dollars?" "No! 50 thousand!"

"How much is your hospital bill?" She asked.

"36 thousand,"

"Keep 36000 to pay your bill, and give me the rest. I have some use for it, after all, I have to pay my movers," and she laughed, as she heard him sobbing, thanking her, and asking "You, you do this, really?"

Her "When you get the money, pay your bill first, bring me the rest." was answered with more sobbing sounds of, "sank yous" and more "sank yuuuus!" as he was freaking out, because he had planned to go to bankruptcy court, as he just didn't have the money for the hospital bill and those collectors had been after him for going onto eight weeks now. As he hanged up, Roxi got ready and started to pack up more staff for The Place, for Richard and Carolyn to share with the homeless people. It was in the early afternoon that Chris stopped by and showed her the receipt where he had paid $35995 at the hospital, and then he was starting to empty a manila envelope to count out the remaining

$14000 dollars. Roxi stopped him, put it all back in the envelope, saying, "I trust you. That's going to be my vacation money when and if I travel to Denmark."

Chris helped her to load up her VW bus with those boxes, clothing, kitchen utensils, and camping gear bought many years back and never used. Soon the car was filled, leaving just the driver seat empty. He greatly admired this lady, herself having little but giving so much. Chris didn't understand her thinking or the idea of giving freely from what you find, so you have space for all those gifts still coming your way.

Chapter 20
The Move

Roxi was loading her Mathilda. With Chris's help, who carried down the stairs boxes and boxes of household goods, the camping gear, and more clothing, it didn't take long. After Chris had left, Roxi returned one more time to her old apartment, getting a handful of cash, five or six hundred dollar bills, and put them in her pants pocket, and she was ready to go. Arriving at the street leading to The Place, driving real slow, picturing where she may have put her tent, looking at where she may have parked her Mathilda, to sleep in at night, she realized that there was only very little place available. At The Place, again she parked right in front of the door, Carolyn saw her coming, seeing the tent gear, the pots, and pans, she was sure that Roxi came to live for good on the street, as expected. "Oh my dear, I don't know where we can get you squeezed in, along the road, let me get Richard, I know he can help you!"

As Richard appeared, he only asked, "So is this all your stuff, or is there more?" As Roxi looked at both Carolyn and Richard, she realized that arriving in an overloaded car, seeing all those belongings, they got the wrong impression. After one more "Don't worry Roxy, it's all going work out, we help you, we are here for you!" from Andy she had met the other day, as well as Dorothy's "Trust in God it's all going to be okay," Roxi was shaking her head.

She looked at Carolyn, and seeing the question mark on Richard's face, thinking and planning her future as a homeless woman. She was smiling when she announced, "No, it's not what it looks like. I got a place to live, miracles happen..."

Seeing the blank stares, turning into smiling faces, Roxi added: "The stuff in my car is for you and those people who need it, it's some of the extra items I am not going to move to my new apartment." Many hands helped her to unload the VW bus, joy and laughter, and congratulations from many people who were happy that things were working out for her. Roxi was surprised about how much love there was and how much people who have so little, care about others.

Roxi had a cup of coffee with both Carolyn and Richard, as Andy and Dorothy were handing out items from the Free-4-You corner. Naturally, they wanted to hear the whole story about Roxi's seeing Ellen, who then set the wheels in gear to get her city housing. As they sat at the round table, Roxi, got to watch people who went to the Free-4-You area and left with items just arrived and donated by her. Without seeing it, she wouldn't have realized how useful some of her hoarded junk was, to those who needed it. In leaving Roxi remembered that she brought cash as well, she handed the crumpled up bills to Carolyn, who gave her a big hug, before handing the money to Richard "We can buy the meds for Maria?" As he nodded his head, Carolyn explained: "...she doesn't have any money, but needs meds..."

*****

Happy, singing to the iTunes music playing on her iPhone, Roxi drove home. It wasn't until she got home that she realized the folded up paper under her right windshield wiper. "Oh shit, a ticket!" she said as she removed it from the car. Opened up in some kids writing it said: "To my angel, thank you!" Expecting a parking ticket, but getting a 'thank you note' made her tear up.

The next days were filled with moving all that was going to stay, including Fred's trunk, into the middle of the spare bedroom to be hauled away by Chris. The living room she used to stack up additional items. All to be donated to The Place, and to her homeless friends.

She boxed up items to move by herself, yet soon realized that putting moveable items in bags was much easier carried down the steps of her old place and up the steps at her new apartment. Well, she learned fast, and yes, she did several trips a day bringing kitchen items, clothing, books, the laptop, but not the iPad over to her new place. Roxi had high respect for the new tablet since she had discovered that those two, her iPhone and iPad in secret, were communicating with each other. Pictures taken on the iPhone showed up on the iPad. The address book from the iPhone suddenly was also available on the iPad. Yes, not having done much with it except checking the mail, she had admired the valuable qualities of the built-in artificial intelligence, including that the tablet listened to being called Siri, just like the smartphone.

She moved all her bedding, her towels but one, and her shoes except two pairs of black work shoes, and the slippers, all her skirts, blouses, and pants except one work outfit, and yes all her under-thingies, bras, socks and jackets.

She did several trips each day, getting more and more used to be home at her new apartment, yet returning to a place which was no longer home, now a place she was eager to leave behind. During her three split-shifts, she slept in a sleeping bag, as all her bedding was already at the new place.

The day before Chris moved her, Roxi made two more trips to The Place, to see Carolyn and Richard. She felt very welcome, not only by those two, but the homeless community and left with feeling high, being happy, without having taken any uppers, knowing she did the best she could to be of service to her fellow men. How true, she couldn't provide a home to the homeless, unable to give what she didn't have, yet had made every attempt of sharing whatever she had to share to make life easier for those less fortunate folks.

By the day that Chris and one helper arrived, left for him to be moved were: Roxi's California King Size bed, one bedside table and mirror, a living room wall unit, a large table, a side table, bookshelves, and six chairs. As well as boxes with whatever she hadn't moved yet in her VW bus. Within hours it was all moved out of the old place, into the new place. As Roxi was putting things away, filling the shelves, making her bed, in her new home, Chris was hauling whatever was left at the old place, to the dump. Chris had asked if he could also come the next day, for half a day or so to spackle the holes in the walls, and do a little move-out paint job. Not thinking much about it, Roxi had said "Yes. That would be great." The next day as Roxi started to wipe down the bathroom tiles at the old place, Chris showed up with two guys and told Roxi "I owe you so much, allow me to take care of the move-out cleaning." She had plenty of things to do and therefore gladly left such up to him. Coming back in the late afternoon, Chris and his crew were packing up. The old apartment had never looked as good. Fresh paint, sparkling clean bathroom, and kitchen, he even had replaced the stove's burner plates. He thanked her, not without making sure she knew he was deeply indebted to her, for being so generous. No, he didn't want any money, not for moving, not for painting or cleaning. "You already overpaid me, Miss Roxi" was his answer to her question of "How much do I owe you?" He left, and Roxi walked around looking at the apartment walls and ceilings, feeling sad, feeling bad for the MacMontry family who used to own it, knowing they would be thrilled to see the apartment the way she left it. Then she went home, her place, the apartment she rented from the city.

*****

Next morning Roxi searched and found the 60-day notice to vacate, gathered all keys, from the old place and drove to Steve's office. It was the same young lady at the counter, the one who had initially confirmed that Roxi had to leave, the sooner, the better. Roxi dropped the bundle of keys: 1 for the apartment door, 1 for mailbox, and 1 for laundry room, all on the desk space infront of the woman.

by helmut s.

Roxi's "I need a receipt for those keys!" showing her the 60-day notice to vacate didn't do much except getting her a "What can I do for you today?"

Roxi's temper had reached a boiling point, and her "Don't you understand English?" was not sounding polite at all. The door to Steve's office opened, Roxi grabbed the paper and the keys, throwing them at Steve, who was still good at catching. Roxi's "Shove them up wherever they may fit, and yes, I have left your uncle's place and plan never to set foot onto any one of your properties."

He laughed, seeing her in her best furious witch role..., ...Steve found her to be funny and didn't take her seriously. With a, "Don't forget to send me the one-month rent deposit, within the month, otherwise, we may meet again, in court," she turned around not listening to his "Wait, just wait a moment Roxi, don't be this way...!" Roxi slammed the door shut behind her as she left the office. Feeling done, done with another part of her past, looking forward to the future, finally she felt being free, happy, joyous and relieved of the yoke tying her to Steve and his uncle.

*****

After Roxi stormed out of Steve's office and drove off, Steve stood at the window. He was steaming, and making plans to get even with this Roxi 'c.nt.' Then Steve saw the Bentley, he recognized Joannie, Roxi's Joannie, driving by and up to the Automobile Associations office. Just seeing her, gave Steve the chills, he had heard too many bad things about her.

Thinking "this 'b.tch' is too powerful and getting on her bad side, you ain't going to do any more business in this town, provided you are still on the upper side of the grass." Steve told his secretary that he had to go to an appointment, and plans to be back later in the day, otherwise in the morning. And with this Steve left his office through the back door, sneaking out, going into hiding, he knew that any confrontation with Joannie would end in a disaster, there was no winning possible for him Mr.Steve G.D. Zilla.

Chapter 21
Freaking Out

It was about fourteen days since moving into her new apartment. She was getting used to the luxury of having a place to call home. At work at the La Casa, she was now scheduled for five lunch shifts a week. No dinner, unless needed for a party. The five lunch shifts guaranteed her at least 30 hours, and benefits. When she saw that the other waitresses Allye and Hilda were also working luncheons, she realized the way male human intelligence works.

The owner and the manager most obviously felt that having men at night for the dinner crowd looked better, and female servers are the ideal luncheon waitresses, as they were a common sight anywhere every place in town.

The Sassy Station & Bar suddenly closed down. The Word was that ABC, the Department of Alcohol & Beverage Control had something to do with it. Yet nothing more was known, the local gossip news had no further information yet. Then Roxi saw Dan, who used to manage the Sassy Station & Bar, downtown at the Farmer's market. He took her aside, thanked her for being a friend, letting her know, "Ventura my ex-boss is in big trouble with the law, but as he has plenty of money, and the best lawyers money can buy, he will make out okay." Then taking her aside, like trying to make sure nobody hears his news, "But listen you may not know, the real reason Steve sent you the notice to vacate, was that he had made a bet with his uncle. And let me tell you, it was a substantial amount, the bet those two, Godzilla and Ventura, made. Therefore Steve was using every tool and trick, to win. The bet was about getting you in the sack, to see if you are as good as, or any better than Rosa your mother, or your grandmother, Lily, who both used to work at the row."

"Sorry, that I disappointed that prick," Roxi was laughing out loud in total disbelief. "What stupid bastard would threaten to ruin a person's life, just to get his rocks off?"

As Dan went on to start a new job, down at the wharf, Roxi bought some veggies, and fruit, after all, her refrigerator at home was empty.

*****

Roxi had no idea that Joannie her ex-husband was the one who had decided to clean the town of the Zilla monster, relatives and offspring. She had paid detectives good money to get all the dirt available on Steve G.D. Zilla. Because of the bet, and that Mr.Ventura had bragged about the deal he had made with his nephew Steve, as well as Steve has talked to more people than just Dan about getting this Roxi doing whatever he wants her to do, because he knew that her grandmother was a working girl, so was her mother. His telling one of Joannie's informants that he just for the fun of it wanted to see how good she is in bed did get under Joannie's skin. Not that she had any direct ties to her ex-wife, but having the Zillas and the Venturas attacking one of her old friends, she took very personal. How could they dare to do as they did? Joannie did not stop with hearsay, but she made sure both Zilla and Ventura's info was collected and checked against the crime data base, she made sure their computers got picked up and all data was searched for evasion of taxes and fraudulent activities as used in many in their business dealings.

Digging deeper into all business dealings of those two, the number of unlawful activities by both truly stunned her. And pissed off, she was, because, on her turf, none of it was going to happen without her permission. She started feeding any of the gathered information bit by bit to the IRS, the DA's office, to ABC, and the federal agencies in charge of whatever federal crime had been committed. Every day for weeks on end she made sure that they got to feel the heat coming from all sides at them.

"Let's give em hell..." was on Joannie's mind, enjoying the game she played with those two jerks, rectifying her actions by telling herself "...after all, hadn't they started it, by playing games with my Roxi's life?"

*****

Somewhat settled in, the fears and worries had fizzled out. Roxi realized that she owed at least a big thank you to the British woman, the one who had sent her to apply for low-cost housing. She had to see Ellen and let her know about the miracle she had performed, by using all her powers and tools to get her, Roxi, a helpless stranger, a roof over her head. Roxi knew it was by the grace of God that Ellen had been able to prevent Roxi from sleeping in her car and living on the streets.

A most grateful Roxi, a $250 dinner gift certificate in hand, compliments of Hans from the Triples Hotel to be used at the Restaurant, Coffee shop or Bar, went to see Ellen. The same office, another woman, turned out to be Ellen's sister, who had been on vacation in India, the home of their family. When Roxi heard that her 'Guardian Angel Ellen' had passed on into the afterlife, she had died a few days ago. Roxi broke out in tears, uncontrolled sobbing she tried to tell Ellen's sister what Ellen had done for her, without even knowing her.

Ellen's sister with a "Never mind, that's what Ellen has been doing while we lived in the UK, and again here. She knew she was dying, had been sick for years, but instead of thriving on her demise, worrying about her own expiration date, she made it her daily job to touch the lives of others and help them to have a better life."

"Really?" was all Roxi could say.

Ellen's sister reconfirmed what she had said: "Ellen believed in doing good while waiting to die!"

*****

It was a few months later, after the main tourist season, that Roxi got an email from Bernd. Yes he had arrived in Dubai, a week earlier, and yes he was taking over a world-class restaurant as the Maître de. Her email to him said: "Congratulations I am leaving for Europe, to stay with my Danish friends in Copenhagen for a week or two."

Leaving Mathilda at home, Roxi was being dropped off by the Airport Limousine at the San Jose airport. Here she grabbed a newspaper from a kiosk to read on the plane. And she did open the newspaper somewhere over Greenland. There was a picture of Steve Godzilla's uncle, the heading saying Drug Smuggler arrested. The article was about Mr.Ventura whose plane had been used to smuggle cocaine, and other drugs into the country. The investigation included his outlets including an infamous nightclub and bar, the Sassy Station & Bar, and several members of his extended family.

On the way to Denmark looking out the window at the end of the wing, she imagined seeing angels flying with her. And the lead angel was Ellen, "... did she have to die, to live on forever?" And then she slept several hours dreaming of an angel by name of Ellen.

She woke up feeling refreshed, went to the bathroom, returning to her seat, Roxi felt like tripping out. She was happy joyous and free to say, "It's so freaking beautiful, the earth is round, any which way we go, what goes around, comes around!" Looking in her wallet, she had a $5000 credit card, secured by her Chase bank account, using the money from Fred's gun. Then there were 2000 US dollars and the 500 Euro, she still had from his Excellency, from the La Casa VIP party. And Roxi felt vibrant, ecstatic, looking forward to seeing her friends Freja and Claus.

At the 'Kopenhavn's Lufthavn' arriving in time, after all, it was a Lufthansa flight, customs and immigration was a snap. Walking into the airport, Claus greeted her, and a young man in a chauffeur's outfit offered to handle her luggage and bring it to the house. She left it totally up to Claus, who next asked her not to be upset because of Freja's arranging a welcome party.

"What party?" Roxi wondered.

"A book signing party!" Claus answered as he steered her to a welcome area, where Freja waited at a desk, with hundreds of copies of a book Roxi had never seen before, and a line of people applauding her, Roxi, upon arrival.

She picked up a book: "The title was Lily, by Roxi a waitress."

Freja let her know that the English version was hers, the Danish version was the translation as done by her Freja, not only an agent, but a well-known writer in Denmark.

Roxi had to sit down, Freja handed her a pen, and she started signing her name until her hand was tired. And a few more, as Freja stood next to her and did all the needed translating...

Now if that's not something to freak out over, what is...???

The night after her arrival at Claus and Freja's estate, in the guesthouse, in a regular size bed, under two feet of eider-down-bedding, Roxi dreamed she had died and went to heaven. And then she woke up, showered got dressed and joining her friends in the kitchen. One boiled egg in a cup, bread, butter and marmalade, was not what Roxi expected as breakfast, neither was the publishing contract with the potential of a steady income for years to come into old age, Freja proudly presented her with.

*****

FREAKING OUT